THE
SCORNFUL
MOON

Maurice Gee is one of New Zealand's best-known writers. He has won the James Tait Black Memorial Prize in Britain and numerous awards and prizes in New Zealand. He is the author of both adult and children's novels, including the award-winning trilogy *Plumb*.

WITHDRAWN FROM STOCK

Also by Maurice Gee

NOVELS
The Big Season
A Special Flower
In My Father's Den
Games of Choice
Plumb
Meg
Sole Survivor
Prowlers
The Burning Boy
Going West
Crime Story
Loving Ways
Live Bodies
Ellie and the Shadow Man

STORIES
A Glorious Morning, Comrade
Collected Stories

FOR CHILDREN
Under the Mountain
The World Around the Corner
The Halfmen of O
The Priests of Ferris
Motherstone
The Fireraiser
The Champion
Orchard Street
The Fat Man
Hostel Girl

THE
SCORNFUL
MOON

A moralist's tale

0405140

LIMERICK COUNTY LIBRARY

Maurice Gee

faber and faber

First published by Penguin Books (NZ) Ltd in 2003
First published in Great Britain in 2003
by Faber and Faber Limited
3 Queen Square London WC1N 3AU

Printed in Australia by McPherson's Printing Group

All rights reserved

© Maurice Gee, 2003

Maurice Gee is hereby identified as author of this work
in accordance with Section 77 of the Copyright,
Designs and Patents Act 1998.

This book is sold subject to the condition that it shall not, by way of trade or
otherwise, be lent, resold, hired out or otherwise circulated without the
publisher's prior consent in any form of binding or cover other than that
in which it is published and without a similar condition including this condition
being imposed on the subsequent purchaser.

A CIP record for this book is
available from the British Library

ISBN 0–571–22166–1

2 4 6 8 10 9 7 5 3 1

One

I wanted a neat bullet hole and no more than a trickle of blood. It fitted with my notions of politeness if not with my understanding of death. There would be no pain of a physical kind, and as for mental anguish and dark ways where the beast might lurk, we would discover those as we went along and shine on them the healthy light of reason, I said. Let's keep it clean, a nice quick murder, or two, or three — there's no harm in multiplication. As for plot: a twist and a double twist incorporating that dark place if we light on it (laughter), but nothing Viennese, we'll keep away from sex, there's altogether too much of that sort of thing.

My collaborators nodded and quaffed their ale. A gunshot in the night. A corpse slumped over his desk. A modicum of creeping on dark stairs, a sufficiency of chasing and close shaves. The heroine in danger (of course). A sensible policeman who likes his pint of ale. The victim? Let's start at the top. We'll murder the Prime Minister. (Won't mention his party. Ha ha.) Or Minister of something anyway. A cold fish, teetotaller, with a frosty wife and a pretty daughter — Jennifer will be her name, she's not the flapper type, we can do without silliness. As for the killer: a prominent man, plain to see while hidden away. He's smiling and unsuspected, but drops a single clue — not handkerchief, not cuff link, some word he shouldn't know — for the clever ones. Let's keep his motive above board in the psychological sense, while his actions are unforgivable, and cruel of course, as murder is. That's agreed? And do you agree to some love interest too, a spot of dalliance for the distaff side? Why not? It's bound to help sales. The pretty daughter and a young reporter, the sort of cub we'll lick into shape.

Myself when young, we said, smacking our lips, filling our pipes.

So we began, not much more than a year ago, and completed nine chapters of the misconceived thing. It's put away and never mentioned. When I run into my fellow plotters in the street we nod and pass by or speak of politics and the weather.

My story is made up of the other things that were going on.

I cannot, even now — my decision made — go headlong at them. I cannot hold them still, look at them and say, This happened, and that, because of a fault here, an easy way preferred, and there a choice made for the best of reasons, feeding a hunger not understood, barely recognised. Moral obligations are turned about and in the end evil, yes evil, is unleashed, and lives are lost, in divers ways, and lost too, forever, are the certainties with which we comfort ourselves.

So I ease my way in, another reason being that I cannot bear to stand alone, even now when I have seen how all of us are alone. I cannot bear my weight of loneliness, but pick up this voice and that, this smile, that laugh, the pipe smoke, the tobacco smell, the taste of ale — the amber liquid, yes, we called it that. I give myself a base of ordinariness, and orneriness too, of human foible and of friendship.

Roy Kember was there, my dear friend Roy, and Euan Poynter, a friendly acquaintance, who calls himself a belletrist and lifts himself a little too high for my real liking, and Marcus Waller, a librarian and, more modestly than Euan, a 'scribbler', and Theo Mead, who filled the back pages of his *Railways Magazine* with comic sketches rather too broad in their humour for me, and Fred Scanlon, an agricultural journalist, and half a dozen others, would-be or failed novelists and story writers — good fellows, most of them, and able men.

It wasn't all pretence and satisfaction.

These paragraphs are like a stone lobbed into a pool. The ripples widen out and if I travel with them from the centre I'll meet whatever stands in their way, rock upraised or floating log, where a counter-ripple begins its journey back. I'll come back too, at my own pace, finding my way.

Eric Clifton said to me, 'Why shouldn't a scientist try his hand? I might bring a new dimension, Sam.' He pointed out that he had published more books and articles than all the rest of us put together. Now he wanted to try writing for fun.

We invited him along and he enjoyed our meetings, smoked his roll-your-owns and once a cigar, laughed a lot, pointed out mistakes good-humouredly, drank his bottle of 'the brown stuff', read his chapter, accepting criticism with good grace, promised corrections, volunteered to advise on gunshot science, medical science, all science, helped smooth ruffled feathers and was a good fellow generally.

That is Eric: a man heavy, water-logged in appearance, yet light and airy in his mind. I lift him out of that company and put him down — put us down — at the point where I can begin.

There are three of us married to three sisters. Men of diverse temperaments, with interests overlapping here and there, although each in his centre stands far from the other two. We're equal in ambition, unequal in the clamour we make and the light we shine. Primacy is granted to James Tinling, although he's several years younger than me and, unlike Eric (his junior by five years), has no reputation outside New Zealand. James makes a gentlemanly clamour, but throws light of a penetrating kind, illuminating that most important arena, politics. He married first and, many would say (although not Eric and I), married best. Violet was his bride — the lovely Vi, ethereal and docile at once (a curious combination), and frantic, baseless, behind her beautifully structured facade, when the deference paid her beauty began to fail. She had thought it was forever but when she encountered the daily circumstance marriage insists on she entered time, an element she had not noticed before and perhaps not even heard about. Violet's beauty was her curse. She floated down time's river like the Lady of Shalott.

Vi had that effect on me — brought out comparisons and evasions. I'll try not to be sad for her wasted life, which began as much in cruelty as silliness. She had a strong awareness of herself, and as a girl would not let the tiniest mark of generosity show in case it detracted from her status, 'the beautiful one'. Ask Rose, ask my wife, who had the good sense to laugh at her and step aside.

The young solicitor James Tinling married Violet Barr. I had met her sister Rose several times but did not know her well enough to be asked to the wedding, and Eric was years away from meeting May — ten years old, a flower girl — and so could not mar appearances with his bearish presence. It was, I am told, a brilliant occasion, for Violet was the prettiest girl in Wellington and James was a cricketer of renown, his father a prominent banker, his mother a leader in society. The wind, not invited, stayed away, and the sun, knowing its business, flooded the city in its bowl with warmth and light — this happy little city that framed the young couple so beautifully.

I must stop this. I do not want to go back all that way. I'll find myself stuck fast — a fly on fly paper — making a futile buzz, doing the 1890s while 1935 escapes behind my back.

I had meant to start with Eric, for safety's sake, but safety's not a way I can take if I want the truth — whatever it turns out to be — so I'll choose another occasion, a beginning that we all make a part of, where the sun shone too and the wind stayed away. No more looking over my shoulder. (The past looms like a towering cloud, joined to us by misty filaments but kept at bay — parenthetically — if the figure holds.) James is our 'host'. He chooses formal language even for our family gathering.

New Year's Day. Eric and May called for Rose and me and we drove out to the Hutt Valley in his clanking Dodge car, which he wished would break down so he might have the pleasure of lifting the bonnet and doing repairs. He never learns to call a mechanic — and proudly shows the crooked thumb broken when his first car backfired while he cranked the engine.

Rose, beside me in the back, asked May if she had seen Vi recently, but May hadn't. Both, they agreed, were on holiday from Vi now that Charlie was home from London to do the nursing.

'I never thought Vi would be pleased to see Charlie back,' Rose said.

'Well, is she?' May said. 'You can't tell. Working out what goes on in her head is like sitting on a branch that's going to break. That's if there's anything at all.'

'Poor Vi,' Rose said.

'Poor Charlie.'

'Amen to that,' Eric said.

I was curious to see sympathy turned in that direction, for it seemed to me that Charlie was doing no more than she should. James had a right to summon her home after supporting her in what he called her gallivanting, and, more severely, her daubing, for how long? — I worked it out, nine years. He had seen no return in the shape of presentable work. And a woman in her thirties, still unmarried, had a duty to nurse her sick mother — even if, in Charlie's case, her mother had never shown her any affection. Rose believed Vi could not forgive Charlie for her imperfect nose and too wide mouth and too small eyes; that she had demeaned herself in bringing a plain daughter into the world.

I had been pleased with Charlie when she was a child. Later I found her far too serious about her painting, but May and Rose corrected me. Why shouldn't women paint and be serious? Did I think they were merely for decoration? For housework and breeding? For stroking your poor brow? They, Alecto and Megaera, were set to go on, but I stopped them by saying that Charlie would do better when she learned not to leave beauty out.

'Beauty!' May said, with scorn. 'Yours aren't the only pair of eyes.'

That argument took place (it went on heatedly) in the year Charlie sailed away, 1925. Another like it seemed likely in the car (nine years had made Charlie even more proficient at leaving beauty out: she goes where the winds of Paris and London and St Ives blow), so I remarked on the importance of the year beginning, of the election that must be held before the end of it, and of the changes it might bring. It was better to have May busy with politics than family — but I had misjudged things, for she said, 'You've heard about James's latest stupidity. He's talking about standing again.'

'It's a brainstorm,' Eric said. 'It won't last.'

'Yes it will. You don't know James: "By gum, I'll show them."

He's practising the common touch. He hasn't said "by gum" since he was on the hustings last time.'

'The age of the gentleman politician has passed,' Eric said.

'James was never a gentleman. Not in politics,' I said.

'Or in business,' May said.

'I don't think he's got the energy for that sort of life any more,' Rose said. 'Can't someone talk him out of it. It's not fair on Vi.'

'He's got the cunning,' Eric said. He smiled at Rose in the rear view mirror. 'Don't worry about Vi. She'll survive.'

'With a bit of help,' May said.

So we came back to Charlie, but also came to James's gate and turned into the long drive and stopped by the front door, where Eric let us out. He nursed his car out of sight beside the garage.

The house was open so Rose and May and I crossed the entrance hall and went past the kitchen, where May popped her head in to talk to Mrs Hearn, who did the cooking. The sound of a tennis racquet whacking a ball, Freddie Barr's cry, 'Good shot, Elsie,' made Rose throw me a grin. I had left my sandshoes at home purposely. Eric had brought his, and the white trousers and sun visor James liked to see, everything correct, although Eric's idea of tennis was to hit every ball as hard as he could for the one spectacular shot in ten he made. James had nick-named him, sourly, Big Bill, after the American tennis player Bill Tilden.

The scene was English, made up: wicker table, sun umbrella, rose garden, lawns and tennis court, four players in white, a woman reclining on a chaise longue. She slanted her cheek for kissing. I ignored it; Rose obliged, then gave the searching look that Vi required.

'Some colour in your cheeks.' (It was most likely rouge.) 'Have you been eating?'

'I managed a little bit for lunch.'

Eric arrived round the side of the house. Vi winced at the sight of him. 'Food is so . . .' She waved her hand limply. A barrier like an order of being stood between Vi and sustenance. She nibbled privately in her room, but with others watching would take no more than a sip of water, with a drop of port wine turning it the lightest shade of pink.

Eric dabbed his mouth at her cheek, missing by the statutory sixteenth of an inch.

'You're blooming, Violet.'

She gave a tiny smile, denying it while pleased to be the centre of attention. I turned away to watch the tennis players, who were James and Charlie against Freddie and Elsie Barr.

As well as cricket for New Zealand, James had played inter-provincial tennis for Wellington. Now, with his springiness gone, he was like a pale stick insect on the court: arms and legs half-folded, body on a sway. He went left or right with a jointed step and blocked the ball neatly between his opponents.

'Oh, Freddie,' Elsie said crossly. In spite of her chubbiness, she's a good player too, as quick as a guinea pig in her movements. Sometimes she could beat James at singles — not surprising as she's younger by twenty-five years. Elsie had been almost a child bride, eighteen looking twelve and blushing plum-red in her peachy cheeks, when Freddie, dashing and middle-aged, married her. By the end of their honeymoon she had learned to scold him.

James saw me watching and saluted with his racquet. 'Shan't be long, Sam. One more game.'

'Sez who?' Elsie said.

Eric came to my side. 'Lob him, Elsie. Make him look into the sun.'

'Eric,' Charlie said — a greeting. I wondered why she had not greeted me. It was her turn to serve. She managed it like pat-ball. Charlie had relearned tennis since coming home but had not done it well enough to satisfy James, who cried, 'Toss it, girl. Toss it high.' He gave her a lesson before she served again — a double fault.

'Told you,' Elsie cried, hopping excitedly on her plump legs.

I turned away, not wanting to see Charlie humiliated. She's quick and competent in things that interest her but when her mind baulks her body dithers: a flutter of indecision in her hands, hesitation, stumble-footedness — and, in tennis, a loosening in her wrist that sent the ball into the net or floating like a butterfly for Elsie to smash. Why didn't she say, I've had enough of this? She has the strength of mind for it. But her father pressed her down. If she were a man I'd say unmanned her.

I went to the table and poured myself some lemonade. Except for Vi's drop of port, James ran a teetotal house. The players called back and forth, the racquets made their underwater sound, the ngaio trees at the edge of the lawn nodded like bishops in convocation, the sun beat down, lighting up the roses and shining on a clear stretch of the stream running through the bottom of James's section — and I did not feel the lack of a glass of beer. I'm a connoisseur of beers and author of a manual for homebrewers that has sold quite well. Also, I've compiled a book of frothblower jokes and anecdotes — but enough of that. The day was beautiful. I did not miss my glass of 'the brown stuff'.

May came out of the house with a tray of scones and jam, Mrs Hearn behind her with tea. The players walked off the court and wiped their faces with towels.

'One set all,' James said. 'Eric, do you want to change? You can take Charlotte's place. She's not much help to me today.'

'Eric, please do. I'm exhausted,' Charlie said.

Father and daughter, as dissimilar as greyhound and labrador. And when you consider Violet, how had the parents made this child? She's as thick-waisted as a woman who has borne a family, with arms, hips, legs — how shall I put it? — too prominent, although not in an animal way but, rather, with the weight of clay. One longs for the liveliness her painting inspires in her, making her as shining as the moon. She achieves a kind of beauty from the workings of her mind.

She went into the house to wash and change, while Elsie, breaking into a new sweat each time she wiped the old away, and Freddie — I haven't mentioned him, but one doesn't nowadays, his charm is gone, he's rather like paper that has curled up at the edge — carried their tea and scones out of Vi's line of sight. They were sensitive enough to know how they distressed her.

Eric changed and came out looking like a grizzly crossed with a polar bear. He too distressed Vi, in all sorts of ways — his ploughman's face and thick-fingered hands and hairy forearms, hairy chest too on that day, sprouting like cocksfoot at the throat of his tennis shirt. His untutored voice and wide-open laugh. She would never listen to my account of his distinction — in astronomy, moon studies, popularisation (Eric describes himself as a vulgarisateur, after one of his heroes, Camille Flammarion) — and would not allow his newspaper column any importance, but complained in her boring voice, 'It's boring.'

James noticed her agitation. 'Violet needs to go inside. Girl!' — expecting Charlie to appear when he needed her.

'I'll take her,' Rose said. She joined hands with Vi and eased her to her feet. The chaise longue creaked like stairs, then squealed in its joints as Eric sat down. Rose wrapped Vi's shawl around her shoulders and helped her inside. We relaxed.

'She's no better?' I asked James.

'No,' he said, closing the subject. I had wondered if his reticence about his wife's health was a way of pointing to the cross he bore — had suggested it to Rose, who said no, James was too much the gentleman for that. All he wanted was for Vi not to be noticed.

Reticence and coldness were weapons of attack. The little he said he said precisely, underlining decisiveness by shortness, which he also made the sign of probity — quite a trick, that one. It was only on the hustings that he raised his voice and peppered his speech. He became unconvincing with vulgarisms. In the House he compelled silence, out-waited abuse, said his few words and sat down. It had surprised me when Gordon Coates made him Minister of Lands. 'Lands' seemed too broad and generous for James, who, as lawyer, saw acreages in terms of conveyancing.

He lost his seat in 1928, when Coates and Reform took a beating, and declared himself glad to be 'out of all that dogfighting on the hill'. He was, of course, not glad at all. He went about in what Eric called his pinched-nose state. He held his back straighter and used, if it's possible, shorter words, more dismissively. No, he said. Quite, he said. There was a squeak of pain at the back of it, if you had the ears, and Rose said that James was crying inside. May said his self-conceit was twisted and there was no harm in having it wrung dry.

Seven years later, was he seriously thinking of standing again?

I did not want to ask. I did not even want to be interested; but was sorry for James, who was guilty of misjudgement and, for once, bad taste. But my years in the Press Gallery, sniffing out stories, following leads, had grown a political organ in me that twitched with curiosity whether I wanted it to or not, and I said, 'What's this I hear, James? You're going back for another dose of punishment?'

'Not today, Sam. Tennis today,' he replied. He did not care for my phraseology — which was careless, I agree.

From the day I had first met James, he had flickered between convincing and unconvincing for me. There had been times when my opinions changed simply because he told me they were wrong.

It was not that I believed he had special knowledge as a politician and cabinet minister, although he was privy to things I could never know, but that his certainties rose from a sense of self that overcame mine, unless I was careful. I had to step back and set myself, inducing coldness in my intellect and warmth in my blood to combat his uncombative forward step. He was master of the imperative in his nature, and seemed to have no need to try. But there were times when it fell away, when James became a poor thing, like a tree thin in its trunk and weak in its hold on the soil. You saw him then as bossy, overbred, long in his opinion of himself, short in his sight of other people, and caught in a turning about — mind and body both — that fretted with a sense of deference not paid and ambitions not achieved. Then one might hear that squeak of pain.

He sat in his wicker chair and sipped his tea. Exercise had raised blood in his cheeks. I thought, James is fallen, and did not know which sense I meant it in. I saw that he must try to lift himself and that winning at tennis might be a way of getting in shape for contests in other spheres. I was, perhaps, a little confused and out of my depth; saw Ousted Politician clearly enough but had no more than a glimpse of James as Fallen Man.

Sip sip he went at his tea (while Eric sucked his like a road worker), then he fished a blue handkerchief from his trouser pocket and dabbed his forehead, patted the bony ledges beneath his eyes. Was there moisture leaking from his nose? It was unlike James. He cleaned himself fastidiously.

I have seen other men of his physical stamp lose their handsomeness as they grow old. Their faces, losing flesh, lose definition — the starving dog not doglike any more but only pathetic: is that too strong? I'll change the figure. He had had a youthful handsomeness of the racehorse kind, and the last thought one would have of him now was starved nag, but he had a shivering quality, he was bared and antiseptic — too white in his skin and fine in his hands and clean in his face. His ears sat close to his skull and seemed all cartilage. His nostrils were slashes in a barely fleshed nose.

I am licensed for this civilised violence against him. But James, let me say, was a handsome man. He could make me feel dwarfish and ill-shaped.

'All right,' he said. 'Shall we finish our match? Eric, if you're Charlotte, perhaps you can curb yourself.'

'Wait, I've got to have a wee wee,' Elsie cried. She ran into the house.

'Which gives me time for another scone,' Eric said.

James walked down the lawn and stood with his back to the house. 'Ah, James,' Freddie said, following him. I do not know what he said to make up for Elsie's gaffe, which was more artless than ill-bred. Freddie will try with James, and fail, until one of them dies.

May came out of the house and started clearing the afternoon tea away. It was Mrs Hearn's job but May is Tolstoyan about such things. Rose sat upstairs with Vi, making, I supposed, those little platitudinous bolstering remarks that were all that conversation with Vi could be.

When the two pairs moved on to the court I found myself alone with Charlie. She took Eric's place on the chaise longue.

'Tired?' I said.

'Exhausted. You know . . .' Her gesture took in upstairs and the court.

'How is she really?'

'Unwinding like a clock.' Charlie laughed, not with mirth. 'And he's winding up.'

'Is he serious, do you think? Standing again?'

'Yes, he is. He let it pass last time, in a kind of sulk, I suppose.'

'Achilles in his tent.'

'If you say so, Sam. But maybe not a sulk, a kind of rage, although I don't know, I wasn't here. Now he's turned it round. He behaves as if he hears some sort of call. You can almost see him standing with his hand up to his ear. Don't let's talk about this. I get pulled into it from so far away. I don't mean just coming home, but *far* away. I have to change my nature from butterfly to bee.'

'You're no butterfly, Charlie.'

'No, I'm not. What I'd like to be — a moth. Some sort of plain brown creature that sleeps in a corner and is *left alone*. Oh, listen to me, Sam. You didn't come for this. I'll end up no better than Mother, I sometimes think. Would you like . . . ?'

I thought it was a walk among the roses she offered me but when we reached the end of the gravelled path she turned towards the implement shed built like the foot of an L on the back of the garage. James had allowed her to make it over as a studio and had approved — reluctantly, no doubt — the building of a skylight in the ceiling. Charlie rarely offered to show her paintings but was not coy about them if one asked to see — which I avoided as a rule, because not only did they not please me, they offended me. I have — how shall I put it? — a strong sense of morphological rightness, in hills, in trees, in people, in *all* things, and Charlie and her kind are intent on creating shapes inherently wrong, defying nature. I cannot see it as other than sinful. In her defence I'll say she's not extreme, does not work at the outer limits of this fashionable and cruel — yes, it's *cruel* — madness. Yet she has gone too far for me, and lost the true balance that allows beauty to be found through art.

Sinful is a strong word. I'll let it stand, although plain Charlie, sweet Charlie too — butterfly or moth or bee — was, is, exists, by dint of true affections, in a state of grace. Sin and grace. Strong words, yes, and I use them improperly, but they turn within an orbit — hers and mine, James's too, and Eric's and Vi's, and the other actors in my story — that allows them a kind of propriety.

She had transformed the room that had once housed spades and rakes and watering cans into a bright clean factory of art. Hangings, perhaps Mexican, adorned the back wall, covering the door that opened to the garage. For the rest, it was business: the potting table pressed into a corner where it served, under a new unhooded light, as a bench for the tools of her trade — the brushes, tubes of paint, stacked canvases, virgin still, the pencils and folios and sketch books, and the unshelved stacks of books that told the histories and methods, and reproduced the work, of the great practitioners she believed she followed — on, perhaps, bloodied knees, as the poet says.

Her own paintings stood upright against the wall, most of them face in, two face out. They were Hutt River scenes, moderately pleasing from the distance I looked and in the poor light. The rest were things she had done in London and shipped home. I knew there were naked figures amongst them and was nervous that she would turn them round, but she stepped past her easel, which faced away from me, and drew the curtain back from the small end window, then pulled the cord that controlled the skylight blind and the room was ambered with light.

'This isn't the sort of place you'd find a moth,' I said.

'Oh, forget that, Sam. Come and tell me what you think of this.'

It lay flatter on the easel than was usual, it seemed to me; uncomfortable for working, but perhaps it was her way to paint bent over her work, peering and pricking like an anatomist, instead of in the long-armed imperious way painters take in photographs.

I moved beside her and was shocked, not by method, not by truth,

0405140

LIMERICK COUNTY LIBRARY

for it was true, but by her ability to paint clear-eyed, steady-handed, and show this thing. Which was, encapsulated on the canvas, James and Vi: their natures and their marriage and the ruin of their lives. Yet it was simple and, to the unfamiliar eye, innocent. A summery picture — and she had not yet been home for a summer so the colours came from memory — full of sunlight and dappled shade and flowers and trees and lawn, with the brick wall closing things off beyond the stream. It was paradisal. This garden was made for happiness, although realistic in its constituent parts, entirely so — and James and Vi realistic too.

There was, all the same, something faery-like about her, with diaphanous scarf, yellow and blue, and flowered dress. She lay on her chaise longue as though floating — was there a borrowing here from Millais' famous painting of Ophelia drowning in the stream? Surely that was a work Charlie would not approve of? Vi held a red rose limp-fingered, slanting down. Her face — here the faery likeness vanished, and the likeness to Ophelia too — was emptied out: of vitality and hope, almost of humanity. It seemed like china, a white plate, although a very fine plate indeed — and now I'm reading in, perhaps, instead of taking out, employing my familiarity. Viewed without that knowledge, Vi was prettily done, although in that style of smudge and blur Charlie and her kind will use.

James stood facing away at the very edge, wearing his black suit — politician's, undertaker's suit? At his side a rosebush grew, cruelly pruned. That was all: his fine profile and thin hands and the amputated plant. I had never known Charlie admit meaning into a canvas so plainly before.

I said, 'Black's a dangerous colour, isn't it?'

'It sucks up light,' Charlie said.

'Well,' I said, after a while — one must say something — 'you've got the garden, everything there. It's very pretty.'

'But not painted in the way you like?'

'I have to say, no. You know I can't pretend about it, Charlie.'

'Of course not. But what about . . . ?' She meant James and Vi.

'There's too much there, I think. It's not the way you like to do things, is it?'

'No, of course. But how else?'

'And it's rather cruel.'

'I know that. But how do I show what's going on here? The thing that's happening in this house? Oh, this is no good. I'm not blind, I can see. It's a bad painting. I hate it. And no one's ever going to see it, Sam. I shouldn't have shown you. I'll take it out and burn it in the incinerator tonight. But I had to paint something like that, I had to say.'

'Show Eric, see what he thinks. And burn it after that. I think that's best.'

'I hated doing it. I hated it. I felt as if they were squeezing me. Usually I can come in here and what I do — it turns me away from them, I can see without them getting in the road. But I had to do that.'

I make her sound hysterical. She was calm.

'So now it's done, are you all right?'

'As much as I can be. I'll just cover this.' She threw a piece of cloth over the painting. 'What will happen to them, Sam? Mother and Da?'

'They'll go on. There's nothing new.'

'Yes there is. I thought that too, they'll go on, but since he's decided to try for Parliament again it's as if he's set something free in himself. He's opened up a room and let something out. He's got other rooms, Da has, and some of them with things in them that aren't very nice. Stop me, Sam.'

'How? Why?'

'Tell me I can go away from this.'

23

'You can, you know, any time, Charlie. James has got plenty of money for a nurse. But . . .' I wanted to know what she meant, a room opened up, and what she'd seen, or sensed, emerging. 'James has always been ambitious. And at his age — I'm there, you know — you can get overtaken by a sense of unfinished business. Things you should have done, and still can do. It's no more than that, probably.'

'Did you know there's someone called Oliver Joll who wants the nomination? Da found out this morning. A man came to tell him — on New Year's Day, that's how important it is.'

'I thought Joll might want a seat when he stood down from Council. What did James say?'

'He opened the door and showed the man out. And then he stood still for a while. He said, "Very well", almost as if he'd moved something in his mind, or as if he was bringing it out, or saying he would. I can't explain. I just knew I shouldn't let him see me, his face was so —' she flipped the cloth back from the painting — 'like that, like I've done it there.'

'He probably just meant he'd fight for it. You don't know Joll. He's full of bounce. Big head, big long nose, talky sort of mouth. He rolls out the talk, it's a kind of tide. I thought once he wanted to be mayor — but Parliament, eh? Joll's in his forties. James is going to be too old.'

'Can you stop him, Sam?'

'Me? No chance. Not if he's made up his mind.'

'Eric, then?'

I shook my head. 'James is too snobbish about him. And you know where Eric stands in politics. Why don't you just go away, Charlie? Does Vi really need you?'

'Anyone would do. Other people, we're undifferentiated for her.'

'Yes,' I said, although, trying to comfort her, I might have disagreed — but we were in truth-telling mode. 'What you do is paint. I don't have to like it; others do. Eric likes it, doesn't he? And May? James will use you up unless you go. You'll turn into a moth all right.'

'Two things, Sam.'

'Yes?'

'I love them, you know?'

'Love them from a distance.'

'And I've got no money.'

'Be a charlady then. Or teach in school. Can't you be an art teacher? Or train as an office lady. Anything.'

But I had no answer that would satisfy her love; and none to replace the studio she had made. Whatever went on in the house — or failed to go on — she could come here; whatever James demanded, she could, in the intervals, take her saving stance and paint; take out from her head the thing that moved her, express what she had learned of beauty and truth — cut off from me by the manner she went about it; wash herself clean. Going back then to James and Vi must turn the coloured coat she wore inside out, exposing patched elbows and grey sleeves.

I took all this from her saying simply, and indicating with her hand, 'Where else could I have a place like this?'

'Does James come in?'

'Oh, he looks in the door. Then he frowns and goes away.'

'He musn't see this painting.'

'No, I'll burn it. Will you and Eric try, at least? I just think something bad will happen.'

I promised I would talk to him, and persuade Eric to add his weight. She covered the painting, closed the curtain and the blind, and we went outside. A tennis ball came bouncing towards us and she shot out a hand reflexively, quick as a cat, plucked it from the air and lobbed it back over the wire. Nothing, I thought, could illustrate her hidden qualities better. She was a live person, full to the brim with abilities unvalued in James's house, where she was Girl, where she lay uncoupled from herself. But that's nonsense, I tried to say, Charlie paints in her studio, and she's free. This mewling about poverty and love is something she can cure herself of like snapping that ball out of the air. She can wear her hidden colours turned right way out. No one needs to be a prisoner, we're not back in Victorian days — and so on, rehearsing arguments, while we stood at the court entrance and watched the match progress. Nonsense too, I thought, to talk of James opening a dark room in his head and letting out some creature prisoned there. Oh dear, oh dear. Charlie must get away, we really must persuade her.

'Do you manage to sell any of your paintings?'

'Oh, one here and there. For nothing much. May and Eric bought one.'

'Yes, I know.' I supposed that Rose and I should have one too, but we had no place to hang it where it would not be seen. 'What about showing them? There are all sorts of group shows and exhibitions.'

'I've got some watercolours accepted. I doubt very much . . . forget it, Sam. My sort of painting . . .' She shrugged.

'They're not what people want, I know, but you can paint things that are more popular.'

She looked at me hard. I saw some nastiness — let me say essential nastiness — snap into being in her face, reflexively, like her hand going for the ball. 'Did you enjoy doing your book of jokes? You wanted to write properly once, didn't you?'

She turned and went into the house, and I thought, Well, damn her. How dare she? I wash my hands . . .

Two

Eric and I strolled down to the stream. The dappled shade and moving water put him in Shelley-quoting mood — he will trot out lines, drop them into any pause in the conversation, appropriately, inappropriately, it does not matter. He has a sweet tooth for Shelley and sucks these verbal confections like peppermints; he offers them round. When I described my talk with Charlie he intoned, 'Poor captive bird! who, from thy narrow cage, Pourest such music...'

'Come off it, Eric, she paints, she doesn't sing. James is the one in trouble.' I told him about Oliver Joll contesting the nomination for James's old seat. 'Even if James doesn't decide to try for it himself, he'll never stand by and let Joll have it. And if his name goes forward and Joll beats him...'

Eric turned a wad of mown grass with his toe, then nudged it into the water. 'I'm not sure I'm going to be bothered with James. Everyone studies him too much, we bend like trees. He's not the centre, Sam, he only thinks he is. It won't fret me too much if he gets a bloody nose.'

'James can't stand up to Joll in a rough-house fight. When he gets beaten, what will happen here?'

'He might just turn his face to the wall.' Eric took a crooked step across the stream. He wobbled, almost tipping sideways. Impatient,

29

I gave his back a shove, propelling him to the other side, then, teetering forward, had to jump across myself. He nipped my sleeve between finger and thumb and saved me from unbalancing into the shin-deep water. We had these semi-comic episodes, Eric and I, nearly always brought about by his impulsiveness, and although they ruffled me and turned me squawky as a rooster they also increased my fondness for this awkward gifted man, my brother-in-law; made me, for a moment, protective of him. He grinned at me.

'A good part of James is facing there already,' he said. 'Charlie is the one we should worry about.'

'Did she show you her painting?'

'I nipped in and had a look when I parked the car. It's got a kind of fault line, don't you think? Everything's done in her usual way except their faces. They look as if they're painted on porcelain.' He hacked his heel in the grass like a rugby player preparing to kick for goal — except that he was fretful not calculating. Eric's easy acceptance, calm of mind, his animal contentment, made a rock in our family. We rested there in upheavals and steadied our feet again.

'I don't want to see that girl go under,' he said, and it struck me from a tremulous note in his voice that there was more between Charlie and him than shared ideas. Had he gone further? He saw the question in my face and said, 'I love her like a daughter, Sam, so don't go shooting off.'

'No.'

'But maybe something more than that as well.'

I asked him what he meant, afraid some flaw would appear in Eric to change our lives — May's and Rose's and mine.

'I want to underpin her, Sam. And send her on her way. But go with her as well. Do you see what I mean?'

'No.'

'She's a practical woman. She's matter-of-fact about her painting.

30

Doing it is the thing. Putting on the paint. But I'd like to know what she sees before and after.'

'Maybe not much. She's swallowed the whole caboodle. Distortions and nature out of tune. Red hills and trees like mushrooms and clouds like stones.'

Eric laughed at me, then grew serious. 'Unless she paints it's a wasted life. She's not a weekend dauber. It's something she was born for. I'd like to know more about that. There's James looking for us. From his home among the dead.'

I read a bit of Shelley myself, although I'm out of tune with his excesses and piling on, which are especially damaging in the poem Eric quoted from. Yet he had chosen aptly — poor James in his 'home among the dead' truly enough, with the 'one chained friend' with whom he must 'the dreariest and the longest journey go'.

We jumped the stream and met James on the lawn and found him still contented from his tennis victory, which Eric had contributed little to. He walked with us back and forth, in manly promenade, expatiating on world events: Chancellor Hitler at his nation building, Mussolini plotting empire in a desert waste, and socialist evils everywhere, which would have brought us home to Wellington if Eric had not butted in: 'Do you see what this man Goebbels says about Germans deserving the blessings of heaven? "Hitler is the faith with which we confront trustfully life's asperities." '

'That's blasphemous,' James said. 'Nevertheless, one can't blame Germany, the threats they face. I'm more concerned with our own back yard —'

'Our gigantic cow yard,' Eric said, quoting Massey.

James frowned. He had had no liking for Massey, who failed to promote him, and whom I believe he'd found repugnant: corpulent, farmer-faced, thick-limbed, thick-minded too (James did not say it in those words), a leader unworthy of his role.

'We're more than a cow yard, I think. Although, yes, the Empire's outlying farm. But we won't retain that function long if we allow these socialists their way. They'll bleed the country white in no time, you'll see. Print it and mint it, isn't that their philosophy? Yes Eric, I've heard your arguments, but how you can, an educated man . . . They've never done a day's work in their lives and yet they believe they can put the laws of the Universe at defiance.'

'Well, as to the laws of the Universe,' Eric began; but, 'Such folly,' James went on. 'Bray a fool in a mortar and yet his foolishness will not depart from him.'

Time to head for cover when James argued from the Bible. He became so fine honed with rectitude he cut like a knife — all the slashes shallow and none directed with more than conceit, yet, with their little weight of authority, they could hurt. We might have been in for it, Eric and I, but were saved by an arrival unwelcome to James. With his sharp ears — all his senses, the primary ones, were sharp — he heard the motorcycle before we became aware of it. A spasm of annoyance crossed his face — the shiver, the puckering a sudden wind makes on a winter pond — and he said, 'Now what does he want?'

The young man, grinning and goggled, who wobbled his vehicle along the path between the house and garage, then rode it across the lawn to meet us, was Freddie and Elsie's son, Taylor Barr. He put down his legs, balanced the motorcycle, took off his gloves and goggles and leather helmet, showing bright eyes and brighter hair, and cried, 'Happy New Year, uncles all.'

'Take that contraption off my lawn,' James said.

'Aha. Careless of me,' Taylor said. 'We've had enough oil spills today, haven't we Owen? Uncles, meet my friend, I've talked about him. Owen Moody.'

32

The young man on the pillion seat dismounted and offered his hand. 'Sir,' to James, 'I'm honoured to meet you. We're sorry to disrupt your peace and quiet. And intrude like this. Tay insisted, didn't you Tay?' He wore no helmet or goggles, which seemed to give him candour, perhaps from the nakedness of his face, the dry sweeping back of his hair and redness and wetness of his wind-stung eyes. I shook hands with him after James.

'I've heard of you, haven't I?'

'I don't know. I'm not really known for anything.' He smiled at James — self-deprecation there. 'I have played a bit of cricket, sir. Only at club level. Don't have the eye for it, I'm afraid' — complimenting James. 'Taylor, can I take this bike away?' — this by way of instructing Taylor to move it, which he did, although no further than the kitchen yard, where he turned back.

'Where's my ma and pa, they said they'd be here.'

He went into the house and, the irritant removed (Taylor is Freddie and Elsie mixed, her commonness, his stupidity, with a voice that scares birds from distant trees and a conceit that makes it louder), James relaxed his frown.

'You scored a hundred, didn't you, for varsity?' he said.

'Ah, well, yes. I got dropped on twelve,' Owen said.

'It takes a good player to go on.'

'Now I've got you placed,' I said. 'You write poetry.'

'Verses, yes. In *Art in New Zealand*. I hope to do better ones than that. Professor Clifton —' turning to Eric — 'I'm a real fan of your articles. I read them religiously.'

James was frowning again, perhaps at poetry, which he had no time for, perhaps at 'fan' (I can't say I liked the word myself); and the boy, understanding whom he must please, said, 'As soon as Taylor has kissed them for New Year we'll be on our way. But can I say —' he looked uncertain, and I thought, This fellow can act —

'perhaps I'm talking out of turn, can I say how much I hope we'll have you back again, sir?'

Too many 'sirs', yet I was not certain Owen Moody was in-sincere. There was a charge of feeling in what he said. James felt it too, and although he sent a chilling glance at Owen, merely replied, 'That's not a matter I wish to talk about.'

'No, of course. I understand.'

'I don't want anything getting out. I suppose it was Taylor?'

'He mentioned something, yes.'

'And Freddie told him. You see —' turning to Eric and me — 'how can I be expected . . . ?'

'It'll be common knowledge soon enough,' I said.

But James must control things and punish when punishment was due. 'If you'll excuse me, I'll have a word with those two.' He went into the house.

Owen Moody's eyes were wet, either from the motorcycle ride or mortification.

'I seem to have put my foot in it.'

'Everyone does with James sooner or later,' Eric said. 'What was that about an oil leak? Is that machine playing up?' He had an appetite for mechanical trouble.

'Oh no, he only meant — we've been swimming at Oriental Bay. Oil gets spilled from ships over at the wharves and I came up under a patch of it. I had a kind of grey-brown halo on my head. We had to go up to my flat and wash it out. It took a whole hour and used up just about a bar of soap. It's why he's so late wishing his parents Happy New Year.'

He had an alert sensitivity, signalled in his eagerness to please, and signalled physically by a lightness in his movements that a hard, almost heavy musculature could not weigh down. His face held an uneasy mixture of the coarse and fine — I hesitate to say of the brutish and well bred, both words too blunt at the edge, yet they come to mind. Perhaps if I make an inventory: bony forehead, indented, thumb-dented at the temples; blue eyes, girlish perhaps in their overlong blond lashes; interested, interesting eyes, intelligent, humorous, even when sore with wind and salt, and probably soap, as on that day; but nose, then, thickened at the bridge and fat about the nostril wings — and this, of course, becomes absurd, I'll go no further. How would Eric emerge from this sort of noting down? How would I?

What I knew then and what I know now — how am I to keep them from their adversarial stance?

Owen Moody was pleasant; he was pleasing, let me say. I talked with him about his versifying, persuaded him to drop that classification (quickly done, his modesty was false) and found that he valued his poems more highly than I. He thought of himself as a poet, in fact, not as a clerk — no harm in that — and was armed with a sense of his own worth that would prickle and inflate if given the chance, like one of those rare fish from deep in the sea — porcupine fish, I think they are called.

'Tay mentioned to me — but maybe it's another thing I shouldn't know?'

I asked what — was meant to ask, he managed things.

'He told me about your book. You too, sir,' to Eric. 'The detective story you're writing with your friends.'

'He's got a loose mouth, our nephew,' I said.

Our literary game was something the new men — Glover and his kind — would ridicule us for, and the thought of Taylor hooting it about among his friends filled me with anger and consternation. He presented us as jolly uncles, quaint old uncles, I supposed.

'We're not a subject for conversation any more than James.'

'I'm terribly — I had no idea,' Owen said.

Eric, sorry for him, said, 'There's no harm done. It's Sam's pigeon really and he wants it kept quiet.'

'It's only a game,' I said, then baulked at the lie. It was something I had the highest hopes for, as several of the others had: Euan Poynter, Theo Mead, Tom Gow especially. Eric too, an optimist in everything he took part in, believed we were on our way to competing with the ladies — he meant Christie and Sayers and the new girl, Marsh.

'I'll ask you not to spread it,' I said. 'I've no doubt Taylor treats it as a huge joke. How did he find out?' I turned to Eric.

'From me, I suppose. I was telling Freddie —'

'Eric, didn't we make it clear when we had the meeting . . . ?'

I turned away angrily and heard Owen Moody say, 'I seem to cause trouble.'

'No, no,' Eric said. 'I've got a whole collection of dog boxes, this is one more. Let's not have one of your tantrums, Sam. These mistakes get made. I'll sit on Freddie and Taylor, I'll shut them up. And I'm sure this young fellow . . . ?'

'Yes. I promise. Mr Holloway, I'm positive you think it's more than a game. I mean, I don't think you and Professor Clifton and the others —'

'Did Taylor tell you their names?'

'Some of them. But I'll forget them if you want me to. Look, I know you and the Professor wouldn't waste your time. I'm sure you want to write a good book.'

'You are, are you?'

'And what I thought — I know it's presumptuous of me — but I have published bits of prose as well as verse, you see. I'm not unknown.'

Eric laughed, and I gave a crow of amazement. The fellow was asking if he could join.

'I'm young, I realise. But Thomas Gow is hardly more than thirty and his stuff is mainly verse, isn't it? I can do as well, I know I can. I took the liberty — I realise it's a liberty, but good writing breaks the conventions, doesn't it? — I brought along two or three pages I've written, just to show . . . It's atmospheric. The sort of thing you want when a murder's getting done — dark streets and rain and wet shrubs and all that —'

'The murder's been committed,' I said.

'Windows with broken glass and a door creaking on its hinges —'

'The murder's done.' By me, and thoroughly.

'Yes, Sam, but there's more coming up,' Eric said. 'I'm not sure Theo's got enough ghoul in him for his. Let's see what Owen's written. It can't do any harm.'

Owen had already taken an envelope from his pocket. I refused to accept it. The boy's effrontery had an insulting edge. I sensed in him something watching, adjusting too, behind an ingenuousness that had to be bogus.

'How old are you?' I said, and wondered if he could redden at will.

'Twenty-eight.'

So, no boy. That was bogus too. I wondered what he was doing running about on motorcycles with Taylor, his junior by nine years.

Eric snared the envelope as neatly as he had snared my sleeve. 'We'll have a look. You know, Sam, I'm no writer either, not of fiction, but you took me on and I've done a good chapter, you've admitted as much. All right, too much scientific stuff, but I'll weed that out. And you know Marcus Waller's going to throw in his hand —'

'Is Marcus Waller in? He can't write,' Owen cried.

'Is that your opinion?' I said.

'Sam, come on, put a lid on it,' Eric said. 'Marcus is no novelist.

37

Half of us are not. We'll read your piece,' he said to Owen. 'But mum's the word from now on, all right?'

'Yes, of course. I'll be really quiet.'

So Eric arranged things while I stood silent. Yet oddly enough, when Taylor and Owen had ridden away, his judgement on the newcomer was as uncertain as mine.

'We'll have to keep our eye on that one,' he said.

Mrs Hearn finished at 6.30 so Charlie and Rose and May served the meal. Vi did not come down but had a tray in her room — the tenderest piece of lamb in bite-sized pieces, the smallest potato, and no gravy because just the sight of it made her ill. She tinkled her bell three times during the meal, calling Charlie.

'Girl,' James said, each time it sounded.

'She's not deaf, James,' May said. 'No, sit still, Charlie, I'll go.'

James had a speech in his head about a man being in command in his own home, but did not make it. May outfaced him; she's afraid of no one.

Later, while the women cleared the dishes and washed up, we walked in the warm night, back and forth by the tennis court, four men as mismatched in ideas and interests as any quartet you are likely to find, yet two of us, Eric and I, with a large affection binding us. I smoked my pipe, Eric his cigar, James and Freddie cigarettes — James's a Turkish brand, matchstick thin, a survival from the dandyism (always moderate) he had practised in his youth.

'Now James, come clean,' Eric said. 'If we're going to hear gossip, we need to know how to respond. It's no good just saying, "Don't know." So out with it, man. Are you standing or not?'

'It's unofficial,' James said. 'But yes, I am. That's to say, if I get the nomination.'

'Which you will,' Freddie cried.

'Yes,' James said. 'But it's no thanks...' The meal, the soothing warmth, our company perhaps, had mellowed him. He did not complete the rebuke.

'What's this I hear about Ollie Joll?' I said.

'Where did you get that?' James said sharply.

'It's going around. There aren't any secrets. He was bound to try for a seat. I wonder why that one.'

'He has business interests out here. Also, with these new boundaries, it's safe.'

'Nothing's safe any more. Not with Labour revving up the way they are.'

'And because he thinks I'm...'

'Too old.' Freddie, always foolish, completed what he imagined James had meant to say.

'Forgotten,' James said. He made a sharp-elbowed quarter-turn away from Freddie. 'Joll is a blowhard and a bully.'

'He's popular.' I might as well say it: 'He could beat you.'

James banished me too — another turn. But I was no more prepared than Eric to bend to him: 'You should have stayed in touch, James. Reputations are nothing. Politics can be cruel. You turn away for a moment and, you're right, people forget. Or if they remember, it's for the wrong reasons.'

'What exactly do you mean?'

'Ho hum,' Eric said.

I meant that James owned too much property, had fingers in too many pies: a carbon dioxide and dry-ice factory, a rent-collecting agency, a bottling plant, even an amusement arcade, and — this told most against him — owned two farms with managers running them, farms that returned soldiers had been forced to walk away from. Dudley Aimer (a long-standing friend: he had promised to do the jacket for our composite murder story) drew a cartoon of James thin as a rake, prune faced, hook fingered, with pockets as fat as Christmas puddings and coins and banknotes tumbling out, and although he rarely needed names on his caricatures, supplied one on this occasion: James Tinkling. The name stuck. My brother-in-law was tinkling with gold coins after that.

'There's been a change of mood. But more than that, a historical change. We're not where we were ten years ago. There's a new wind blowing —'

'You can stop the journalism,' James said.

'— and it's made people bend a different way. Yes, all right, journalism, and I'm retired, but don't tell me you don't know it, James. I think this is a good year not to stand for Parliament.'

'Unless you're Labour,' Eric said.

'Labour won't win. It can't,' James said, dogmatic. He gave us reasons — moral not political, he was so out of touch.

Eric walked down to the stream and hissed out his cigar butt in the water. He strolled to another part of the lawn and stood with his thumbs hooked in his waistcoat, looking at the sky.

When the women came out of the house, he called, 'May, turn the lights out for a minute. I'll show you something.'

May turned back, Rose with her, Charlie too, and, as if all three were worked by a single string, switched off the lights. Darkness came like a blow, a blotting out. Then the sky sprang like a tiger: Eric's show.

'Terrifying,' Rose whispered, when she reached my side.

Eric said, with satisfaction, 'Constellated suns.'

'So many,' Charlie said.

'It doesn't do to forget them.'

'Day and night. Always there.'

'Do they have planets, Eric? With life on them?' Rose asked.

'Who knows?'

'Nonsense,' James said. 'Life was placed on Earth by the Creator. Who made His purpose clear. There's no men or anything else on Mars.'

'You're like a fish, James. You can't imagine any other world outside the water.'

Eric speculates a little in his columns but keeps away from extra-terrestrial life, things like that. I was surprised to find him so expansive here; speaking of light years, multiplied — 'Our history, told at that distance, is like the buzzing of the bluebottle fly' — when his real concern, his professional study, is severe and formal, although wide ranging, from the moon (he's world renowned for his work on the meteor impact theory, which replaces the old volcanic belief) to variable stars.

'One of the things I missed in England was the Southern Cross,' Charlie said.

'It's the purest of the constellations,' Rose said. 'The perfect one. But everything is perfect up there.'

'I wish that was true,' Eric said.

We stood silent for a while. I felt drawn out of myself, perhaps we all did, into the immensities of the universe — in a state where questions and answers drift into nothing and only wonder remains; and the eye, that tiny organ, seems not to understand but absorb the mystery.

Charlie sighed, Rose murmured and James said impatiently, 'Is anyone getting cold?'

Far away, Vi's bell made its plaintive call.

'Girl,' James said.

'No, Charlie. You go, James. She's your wife,' May said.

Impossible to see his face, it made a pale blur. 'I can't do anything for her,' he said; then, seeming to hear himself: 'In nursing, I mean. I provide, that's my part.'

'Perhaps all she wants is for you to hold her hand. On New Year's Day. Go on, see.' May is daring, dares anything, but was on top of a volcano now. Charlie started off. May took her arm. 'No, James will go, won't you James?'

The bell rang again. We all, far from the house, felt that we might hear Vi shrieking soon.

Then James said, 'Damn. Damn.' He broke away and seemed to dart, shadowy, to the house. The hall light went on; we glimpsed his back as he lunged towards the stairs.

'He won't hurt her?' Charlie said.

'He'll hold her hand, like I told him,' May said.

'I don't think they've spoken alone for months. Maybe years.'

'Well, New Year, renewal time,' Eric said. 'Now, look here. I'll show you something.' He pointed us at the sky again, facing north, where the Hutt suburban glow interfered less, and showed us a group of stars between the Pleiades and Orion. 'Now up-wards a little bit, to the right, see those stars in a flat triangle.' He might have been showing us microscopic objects on a slide, but equally a view of distant villages where he lived. 'They're Alpha and Gamma and Delta Ceti. Now come south.' He aimed us patiently, produced us from the triangle's longest side until we came to a fourth bright star, close enough to be part of the group yet far enough away to stand on its own. It seemed we could choose.

'If you'd looked a few weeks ago you would have seen only a pinpoint of light. And if I stand you here for two more weeks —' he took May first, Charlie second, by the shoulders, and anchored them — 'you can watch it start to fade away.'

'What is it?'

'Mira Ceti. It'll shine like this for a little while, then take about three months getting dimmer. After that, for half a year, you won't see it at all.'

'Why?'

'No one knows.'

'Oh come on, Eric, surely *you* …'

'Nope. Variable stars get eclipsed by some dark body or other, that's fairly certain, because it takes such a short time, but this — there's no explanation. Mira Ceti shines for a while, then something unknown happens and it fades and goes away.'

'It's spooky. Like ghosts,' Rose said.

'But while it's dark it's still there, doing what it does,' May said, 'so don't treat us like a primer class, Eric.'

He laughed. 'There's a good scientific reason, but no one's found it yet.'

'Charlotte. Girl,' James called from the kitchen door.

'I'll have to go,' Charlie said.

'What is it, James?' May asked.

'I can't do anything with her.'

Charlie crossed with him on the lawn and went upstairs.

'What is it?' May asked again.

'She's crying now. She says she's all alone. She says …'

'Yes? What?'

'She doesn't want this new year.' James shook his head petulantly. 'How can I be expected … ? I need support, not this sort of thing.' But that was enough; he tied himself up tight like a bundle of sticks. 'I'm sorry. I meant us to have an enjoyable day.'

'Come here, James. I'll show you Mira Ceti,' Eric said.

'You can use it in a political speech,' I said.

Three

Three weeks later. The scene: my study.

Not all in our band of scribblers were pleased to see Owen Moody arrive. Roy Kember, especially, disapproved. Roy and I are the relic of an informal club of twenty young, or youngish, men — twenty at its peak — whose business was conviviality. We talked about poetry, music, politics, sport, the woman question, world events, and sang songs round the piano and smoked a lot and drank a lot of beer. Our name was The Frothblowers' Club. To join you must display — in style and conversation — a comic surface and be serious underneath. We had good times until the War decimated us. (Note: 'decimated' used in its proper sense.) Some became too serious after that. Others indifferent. All too old. The Frothblowers' never re-formed. Several among us stayed good friends, but only Roy and I met regularly. He was a waspish man, embittered by his failure to be great. He was ready to sting — a misused word would do it — and his victims were almost always young. I liked him for his honesty and his sharpest sting saved for himself.

What a pity he became a different man when he wrote. I had to cut 'trucidation' and 'lethiferous' from his chapter, and 'Cain' when he wrote of killing and 'Cupid' when of love.

Roy felt we should have had a meeting before inviting anyone else to join. 'Let's hear some of your stuff. Recite it,' he told Owen.

'I don't have it on the tip of my tongue,' Owen said. 'But I gave Mr Holloway some sample paragraphs. I'm happy to read those if you like.'

'Not necessary. They're good enough,' I said.

'I'm sorry if you don't want me, Mr Kember. I'll go if you decide to blackball me. But can I say how much I admire your work.'

'I haven't got any work,' Roy said, liking Owen less.

'We don't blackball,' I said. 'Here's how things stand. Owen came along at my invitation. Eric's too. So you can get a look at him. I've asked him to write a sample chapter. What you don't know is that Marcus Waller has pulled out. So Owen's going to have a shot at his bit. Which he'll read to us next meeting. If we don't like it, he'll go away. All right, Owen?'

'You won't see me for dust,' Owen said.

'Roy?'

'As you wish.'

The others said, 'Welcome aboard' and 'Good to have some young blood', and we settled down with our pints and pipes to hear Tom Gow. His chapter put in twists of plot — creaky, clumsily worked. As for the rest of it — must every hired thug have a scarred face and eyebrows that meet in the middle? I saw tightened lips and downcast eyes, and felt an anger equal to Roy's at words misused.

A smile, a little jeer, showed on Owen's mouth. Tom Gow was 'young blood' too.

'You boys need some lessons in grammar,' Roy said.

So we talked about collective nouns with singular verbs and left the real messes for me to clear up. I took Tom Gow aside and went over the worst. He's a fellow who burns with resentments; I heard the sputter of their igniting as we spoke, and guessed I'd have his letter of default in a day or two. We were going to need Owen Moody.

In case anyone is interested, here's a summary of our story. A gunshot rings out in the night. John Woodley, the dictatorial and unpopular Prime Minister of New Zealand, is found by his secretary slumped over his desk, with a bullet hole in his forehead. His limp hand rests on a revolver, but Inspector Jarvis is not fooled for a moment: this is murder, not suicide. (In Roy's chapter it turns out that he was not meant to be fooled, the murderer required only 'a temporary obfuscation'.) Woodley's daughter, as attractive as he is cold and closed . . .

But I can't go on. Nobody is interested. How did we persuade ourselves to do it? Since Adam's day fools are in the majority, the poet says. Self-importance played a part (that's four or five of us — editors of joke books, authors of dud novels and 'thoughtful' essays and limp poems), ambition too (Tom Gow, Owen Moody), perhaps despair (Roy Kember). Only Eric joined for fun. What a mish-mash we concocted — Cupid, Cain, two Prime Ministers murdered, the second by an undetectable poison, the corpse of a fallen woman in a trousseau box, a motorboat running down a swimmer, a thick-headed coroner, meant to be Dickensian (my chapter, I wrote two), a seedy boarding-house by the Basin Reserve, where a gang of conspirators . . . Enough, enough. The conspirators are fascists, led by the deposed Minister of Finance and a bald-headed mustachioed man with an Italian accent. Enough.

We wrote nine chapters, only one of them any good (I'll come to it), and dreamed of fame and fortune, while smugly dismissing Sayers and Christie and Marsh — 'the knitting circle'. We had no women in our group.

49

They left in two and threes and I called Rose to help me clear away the glasses and ash trays. She held her nose at the 'ugly smell' and threw the windows wide to let in air. Eric carried bottles out by their necks, four in each hand, a barman's trick. He hugged Rose when he came back, whirling her round with flying skirts. They enjoy each other. I'm envious of his ease with women — of his ease with everyone — and awkward, a little, with May, whom I'd like to hug with the brotherly freedom Eric uses with my wife.

'I'll walk Eric up the hill,' I said. (Great walkers, the pair of us, on Wellington's hills, up winding paths and zig-zags and flights of steps, but must look like Laurel and Hardy, I bagging along, he barrelling. Appearances, though, give a wrong impression. I'm prone to anger and squeakiness not tears and Eric is no bully but speaks out.)

We put on our hats and went into the still night, where we found Owen Moody in the street, whacking his hat on his thigh.

'Waiting for my ride,' he said.

'Who? Taylor?'

'He promised eleven on the dot.'

'You'll hear him half a mile away with that open exhaust,' Eric said.

Owen put his hat on and lit a cigarette. He looked like an actor in a movie — flaring match, light on his face, down-tilted brim — like George Raft or the little Irish hoodlum, James Cagney, although he had the features of neither, and I wondered at the warning signs of falseness he produced along with his pleasing openness.

'Mr Kember doesn't like me,' he said.

'Roy's not too fond of anyone.'

'He's sunk in despondency,' Eric said. 'He fires bullets into the dark.'

'Why at me?'

'You showed yourself. You're not the only one he took a potshot at tonight.'

'Just write a good chapter and he'll leave you alone,' I said.

'It'll be hard not to write a better one than Tom Gow's.'

He annoyed me. 'We're not in competition, we collaborate,' I said.

'Would you like me to brush up his stuff?' The easy way he said it, ignoring me while knowing me, increased my anger. Eric's soft 'Ha' added to it. He knew me too: I did not want the job of Tom Gow's chapter.

'He needn't twig,' Owen grinned, suddenly boyish; working, I thought, at repair. He must do it often. 'He was my house captain in the third form at school. He used to whack my bum with the brim of his cap every time we passed. And he wrote no-good poems for the school magazine. He still writes those.'

'I'm not having this turned into a squabble.'

'Twelve writers together, it's bound to be. Here comes Tay.' He trod out his cigarette. 'Don't worry, Mr Holloway, I'll be careful.' He gave a smile — charming smile. 'I'll write you a good chapter too.'

'Yippee-ki-ay-ki-oh,' Taylor sang as he U-turned his motorcycle. 'Lovely night, uncles. I can't take all three of you, I'm sorry.' He pulled goggles from his pocket for Owen. 'Hold on to your hat. I want to break my record going back.' He grinned at us. 'Four minutes from Oriental Bay, how's that?'

'You'll kill yourself,' I said.

'And die with a smile on my face. All set, Owen?'

'Think about my offer, Mr Holloway,' Owen said.

'I sing all the songs that the cowboys know, 'Cause I learned them all on the radio,' Taylor warbled, and roared away.

'Young fool. What does Moody see in him?' I said.

'He's using him for free rides,' Eric said.

We walked along Hobson Street, crossed the suspension bridge and climbed the hill. Eric has a lumpy walk, no ease, no elegance, yet he moves without distress, uphill and down. A long flight of steps will make him pant, but he listens to some counter in himself and slows or quickens as it ratchets up and down. He has the science of it pat, I'm sure.

Usually on our walks we talk non-stop. I might start with a remark about some political event, some medical discovery, some book I'm enjoying, or horse race or mountaineering feat — whatever presents itself — but my talk is a thin stream flowing into Eric's river, which swallows it almost at once. He rolls away with the subject, over falls and rapids, along broad reaches — one could extend the metaphor down to the sea. Once as we stood on the hills by Johnsonville and looked into the scrubby valleys to the north I made a remark about recent discoveries in soil deficiency, and Eric was away, from trace elements to organic chemistry, to the carbon cycle, to microscopy and optics and metrology (with a detour into the standardisation of the Enfield and the BSA inch), to ways of seeing, ways of feeling — I might have left out a step or two — from feeling to judging, and moral judgement, to Lytton Strachey's condemnation of Thomas Carlyle's 'reckless moral sense', and I discovered why for some time it had been his joke to refer to me as Mr Caraway. Strachey likens Carlyle's ruinous obsession to the passion for caraway seeds of some German cooks: whatever the dish, they cannot leave them out.

I protested but laughed too, and felt a secret pleasure at being lumped in with Carlyle. Eric dropped 'Caraway' after that. His joke had run its course.

There was no talk of that sort as we walked up Wadestown hill. My mind was spiky with resentments.

'I'm not going to let him take over,' I said.

'Don't fret about him, Sam. He'll create a bit of bother but he's got a sort of largeness, don't you think? That's worth something. I don't know whether he can fill all the space he wants, that's all.' Eric smiled. 'I don't mind him stepping on us a bit: young men should. They climb us like ladders.'

'This fellow's trying to take too many rungs.'

'You're crabby, Sam. You think this thing is not going to work?'

He had hit on a part of it. As for the other, it had to do with enjoyment. I had written my chapters in a doubling-back, side-stepping, potholes-in-the-road manner that I enjoyed thoroughly after the narrow path of journalism. I discovered a passion for metaphors (and did not always notice when they jumped tracks) and wanted to keep that new pleasure. Impossible to explain it to Eric. Instead I went on about the difficulty of my task as editor. How do you make twelve ways of writing cohere; make twelve villains, twelve heroes, twelve pretty girls fit into their single villain, hero, pretty girl mould? Subtleties of language would have to be discarded; contending epithets chosen between; styles raked flat. I would end with a barrel of compositor's type.

'Put young Moody on it. He'll lick it into shape.'

'No,' I said. 'It's my idea.'

'Slow down, Sam.' I thought he meant my walking. 'We're doing this to entertain ourselves. Isn't that the first thing? After that, if it works it works; if it makes us famous and makes some money, that's extra benefits, isn't it? We agreed on that when we got together. If we start worrying, there's no point.'

He held me by the arm to look at the moon. It made tracks on the water like mother of pearl, picked out sheds on the reclamation and drew the harbour wall in white crayon and black ink.

'The old moon in the new moon's arms.'

'What causes that?'

'Earthshine. Reflected light.'

'We shine on them? Like they shine on us?'

'I like your plurals. Come in for a nightcap, Sam. May's still up.'

She was in the kitchen with Charlie, heating water for a pot of tea. Eric poured two whiskies in the living room.

'What's Charlie doing here? I thought James wouldn't let her go.'

'She needed a break. May went out and fetched her. You know May. The housekeeper's got a sister who's a nurse. She's living in.'

'How long?'

'Oh, a week. Two weeks. We'll see. Water in that? No? Good luck.'

I cannot pretend these conversations are exact but it's better being direct than indirect; it puts me up against things, face to face — as when Charlie, letting her tea go cold, told us, 'Mother can't sleep except in snatches. She rings her bell three or four times every night. She's frightened of the dark, even though we keep the night light burning all the time. She says she sees things moving in the corners of the room, but of course it's on the inside of her head. Because she starts on people she's known, girls at school who were nasty to her — and you as well, May. Rose as well. Not giving in to her makes everyone into monsters. Some little thing like squabbling over a brooch or not getting the part she wanted in the school play — and how could she have the best part? She can't be anyone but herself because there's nothing outside unless it's pointing in at her somehow. Anyway, these things get claws, they fix on her like those little demons in early paintings. Is monsters in her mind saying too much?'

'What's the doctor doing? What medicine?' Eric asked.

'Tablets. Phosphorated iron. Which she won't take. It's nervous exhaustion, he says. And that's supposed to cause some sort of capillary haemorrhaging. These things stop that. And they revive the brain. So he says.'

'He means she's anaemic,' Eric said.

'Which is bunkum,' May said. 'Your monsters were there right back when she was a girl. She was born with them.'

54

'Well, she's sick. That's all I know,' Charlie said.

'We brought you over here so you could take a rest from Vi,' Eric said.

But Charlie could not; could no more be called away from her troubles at home than a dog from its dish of food. Am I saying they nourished her? No, they did not. Magnetism would be better: she was drawn to these things by a force, a fascination (by love?), but went reluctantly, jerkily, then in a rush, the way rusty screws and bent nails move when a magnet comes close.

'She says her throat's too narrow to swallow pills,' Charlie said.

I'd had enough of Vi and asked how James was managing.

'By not being there,' Charlie said. 'Even when he's there.'

I'm irritated by cleverness. 'Meaning what?'

'Oh, come on, Sam, use your noggin,' May said. 'James sees what it suits him to see. He can close his eyes and stop his ears while he's looking straight at you.'

'It's more than that,' Charlie said, then looked about distractedly. 'I feel as if I'm betraying them.'

Eric went to the sideboard and poured a glass of sherry. 'Here, drink that.'

'One for me,' May said. 'It's no betrayal, Charlie. All we want to do is help.'

Charlie put the glass down by her cold cup of tea.

'Sometimes when Mother's bell goes, and I'm sitting with her, I hear him get up from his bedroom and go past the door. The floor creaks. Once he stood there for a while. I heard him breathing. Then he goes downstairs. It's ...' she found her sherry, drank some '... not just sometimes. Every night.'

'That's more than being not there,' May said.

'I've gone down a couple of times when Mother's back asleep. He sits in his study, in his chair. I can see him by his cigarette.

He's got the curtains open, looking out. It's as if he's waiting for …
nothing.' She shrugged. 'Not even the dawn.'

'The night does funny things,' May said briskly. 'You need to see
the sun shine, then they'll go away.'

'Does he say anything?' Eric said.

'He knows I'm there. Just once, he said, "Go back to bed,
Charlotte. I'm all right." At least he didn't call me Girl.'

'And in the morning he's good old James again?'

'Goes upstairs and washes. Comes down, reads the paper. The
usual thing. He works in his study. Then his clerk comes in the car
and drives him to work. It's the same every day. The same forever.'

'No breakfast?' May said.

'A cup of tea, that's all. And another one with a round wine
biscuit if he's still home at morning tea.'

'And no more said about going back into politics?' Eric said.

'Nothing. But he is, because — I think he can't see anywhere else
to go. It's as if, when he was there, at least he knew who he was.'

'I think you're being too psychological,' May said. 'Politics is
about being powerful, and James knows all about that. He wants to
get back where he was. But it happens too slowly, so he sits waiting
in the dark. As for the emptiness, that's his marriage. You can't do
anything about it, so don't try.'

But Charlie would try; and try equally hard to get away to her
painting. The fracture in her mind must hurt like a broken bone. I
thought, watching her, that her face had fined down, she was
prettyish (I'm too fond of 'ish' as a qualifier). Likenesses to Vi and
James were starting to show. I watched Eric too: his need to sit
beside her and pat. May smiled at them — not sadly (she is never
sad) but sympathetically and with a temporising slyness as well.

I finished my drink and said goodnight. Eric walked with me
to the gate.

'I suppose you know what you're doing?' I said.

'Sorry, Sam?'

'That girl is going to get a thing about you.'

'She's not a girl, she's a woman, and one with a mind of her own. As for "thing", she's going to end up far away from me. I want to see she gets there, that's all.'

'Does May know that?'

'You're getting to be a busybody, Sam. Goodnight.'

I called him back and apologised.

He said, 'You can only be honest with May. I don't need explanations with her.'

'Charlie might need them.'

Eric sighed and turned away. 'She's my daughter, can't you see?'

I did, suddenly, and was ashamed. He loved May unbreakably and by habit. Childless, he loved Charlie too, with a kind of desperation because of her unhappiness.

'She's a painter,' he went on. 'You don't agree with that. But these shapes and colours she makes, they don't have to be things you come across every day. They're meant to pick us up and fly with us.'

'I don't know where.'

'You don't need to. She's not telling us something we already know.'

'We know who James and Vi are in that one she did of them.'

He sighed more heavily and seemed to deflate. 'That's a different thing. But it tells us a bit more than we've seen for ourselves. Anyway, I stopped her from burning it.'

'Where is it?'

'Out in her studio. Take it easy — James never goes in. Can't bring himself. I've told her I'll buy it when she's ready to let it go.'

'She'd better not put it in an exhibition.'

I said goodnight and walked home. Rose was in bed, dozing off. 'Cold,' she complained, snuggling down in her own warmth.

Night and stillness worked on me. Eric might see the painting as beautiful, and neutral somehow because of that, but the dying rose, the plant with its fingers cut off, and the china faces, made for me a particular, and a cruel and hideous, truth. It held James and Violet screwed in a vise, with crying mouths.

I hoped that Charlie had hidden it deep down, underneath her other paintings, against the wall. There are truths that even daughters should not reveal — especially, I thought, drifting, sliding, when they're daughters who think they are painters when they're not. She should give up daubing, that Girl. Run away from those crippled beings out there, be a teacher, be a nurse, find a useful occupation, and leave them to their broken lives, which they have learned to endure, their china plate lives . . . Violet on her chaise longue, sliding away, and James, who would be Minister of what? The little Department of James Tinling? He would find plenty there to keep him busy. Plenty of — hadn't Charlie said it? — rooms to open doors to and march in. Let him turn the key and not come out — rule the little empire of himself.

Rose sighed and murmured, 'Stop thinking. Go to sleep,' and I obeyed.

Sleeping and dreaming, though, are different states.

James has always had a life in my dreams.

Four

The *genius loci* of our little pocket of Wellington is politics. The hum of decision-making fills the air, which nevertheless lies still with hidden intentions. There's a quietness in politicians behind their noise. You learn, when you work close to them, if it fills a large place or a small, and also if it's red or black. A mixture of those colours exists in some. They're the difficult ones to understand; they always beat you, like Dick Seddon. He kept a huge quiet place behind his noise. I could never believe it contained anything meant to do us good. Massey was easier — a pinkish uncomplicated man, prone to geniality and unconvincing tempers, with no more than a muttering of uncertainty back there.

I could do them all — Coates and Forbes and Ward and Harry Holland — but they're not my story, which, in politics, is James Tinling and Oliver Joll. It's hard to fit them in a single frame, although they stood together at the end.

I lunched with James at his club, a place that confuses me with relief at not belonging and a wishing to belong. James fits in, how he fits, with his fineness matching the club's understatedness and his importance its leathered opulence. I ate cold beef, he steamed fish. He wanted nothing from me, none of my insider's knowledge — I still had some — but was fulfilling his six-monthly duty to his brother-in-law. Eric had had his lunch the previous week.

We're placed alphabetically in James's calendar.

We took a modest table beside the wall. He asked me if that morning's *Dominion* leader had been mine. (I wrote a guest editorial once a fortnight and a feature article now and then, nothing too political, although I'd done a series on unemployment the previous year.) He nodded approval when I said yes. It had been sensible, he said, one must keep hammering away at these socialists. I had thought I was attacking communism: the way it used people as building blocks for its 'people's state', with no notice paid to what an individual might want for himself. Stalin's henchmen had just detained the physicist Peter Kapitza, Rutherford's colleague, on a visit to his homeland. He must be used to build Soviet science, they said. I found this chilling in its absolutism, and said so at some length, but was concerned to find James crediting me with attacking Savage and Semple and Nash.

I got him off his hobby-horse — half dismounted him — by asking about his political plans. He held up his finger. 'You're privy to something I don't want talked about. When the time comes I'll make my intentions clear. Until then . . .'

'Button my lip? But you know what I think about it, don't you? Eric and I, and Rose and May. You've done enough. You've had a career most men would be proud of.'

He ate some fish — chewed it longer than its softness required. He was damping down his impatience, his anger perhaps, at my compliment.

'If experienced people don't work to control these immoralists, they'll take over.' Then his face darkened with blood. He laid down his knife and fork.

I turned in my chair to see who had come in. The noise should have told me: Oliver Joll. With his barking-dog laugh, he was too loud for the room, and too highly coloured (his colour inside as much as out) for its muted shades, its white-linen table cloths and pale waiters. He entered with a cohort, business friends and Council members, and although engaged in jollity (opponents labelled it Jollity), found James straight off with his pushing eyes. He saluted flamboyantly, then acknowledged me: 'Sam, good to see you,' and passed by to his table in the centre of the room.

James patted his lips with his napkin — small quick movements, showing control — yet I saw his hands trembling as he picked up his knife and fork. He pronounces commination in a cold and minimal way; anathema more strongly, in warmer language, with now and then a swear word that strikes like a spear, coming from him.

That day all he said was, 'I must finish this and go. I can't sit in the same room as that man.'

'Why on earth not? You've sat with worse. You're a politician.'

'Can you do without pudding?'

'No, I can't. I'll stay. I'm surprised you let him drive you out.'

My gibe struck home. But Joll could bring blood to his face; I merely whitened it. 'Are you on my side or his?'

'Neither. I thought it was the socialists you hated. Joll is in your party, whatever you think of him.'

'Not the party I helped build. The man is a liar and a cheat.'

There had been rumours years before of a business falling-out, but I had thought it done with; that their antipathy resulted from opposing styles and tastes and their different grasp on life, and different beginnings (Joll was, he boasted, an engine driver's son), and the south pole and equator temperatures at which they lived. Liar and cheat meant something new.

'You'd better be careful what you say,' I said.

He had control of himself again. 'I'll ask you to stay neutral, at least.'

63

'Of course I will. Good God. But can't you see you're riding for a fall?'

'Nothing's certain. You've been around politics long enough to know. And remember please, I haven't said I'm a candidate.'

'Nor has Ollie.'

The name angered him. 'No doubt with your newspaper friends you call me Jimmie.'

'No, I don't. Calm down . . .'

But he had done his trick of shifting in the blink of an eye – knife and fork down, chair back, a lengthening of his legs elastically, tree-insect style – although he did not forget his duty as host: 'I'll tell the waiter you're staying on. Enjoy your pudding.'

Out he went, neither fast nor slow; had his word, took his hat, was helped on with his coat; and he was gone, leaving a nervous silence, broken by Ollie Joll's laugh – a rich production, greedy now. It put me, suddenly, on James's side.

I'm in a family, I thought sourly, but was excited in my newsman's part by the preliminary dance, the soft-shoe shuffle, I had witnessed in the Jolly Ollie/James Tinkling Show (a name coined by Dudley Aimer, who was saving it for a cartoon as soon as those two came out in the open).

I finished my meal – rice pudding, which I scarcely tasted – thinking of the sad figure James made in Charlie's account, sitting in his study in the dark. She had said he looked at nothing, but I did not believe it. He turned over his unlived life: that's to say, his life in private with Violet Barr. As for his public life, which exercised my curiosity more than my feelings, his wish to start it up again came from desperation. James would leap into the light of day and practise there the certainties he knew, renew himself, while holding at arm's length and making invisible, even to himself, the demons that tormented him at home. I added his ambition (never mentioned) for a knighthood (he already had his MBE). A second term as minister of the crown might earn him that.

I could see James kneeling straight-backed on the cushion, and straightening even more at the touch of the Governor-General's sword, but could not bring Vi into the picture, so returned him to his chair in the dark. He smoked while sitting there, Charlie had said — and solitary pleasures suited him best. In public he lit up only with friends, in uneasy camaraderie; he turned his back on women when they smoked. (May had lately taken to fishing out Eric's tobacco and rolling her own, which so offended James that he had to leave the room.)

I turned these fragments over as I went into the street. It disturbs me how little I knew James.

'Sam, are you going my way?' Oliver Joll came up behind me. He fell in step.

'You've missed your pudding,' I said.

'I wanted to get away from that gang. And have a word —' which would be about James. He put it off as we strolled down to Lambton Quay, and instead praised that morning's leader, which he'd picked as mine. 'You must have lunch with *me* soon, Sam. We haven't had a chance to talk since — when?'

'Akatarawa. At the relief camp.'

'So it was. I thought those articles you wrote were right on the button. Although you must have had to . . . ?'

'Cut my coat? It was the *Dominion*, after all.'

'Owned by a man as fat as those poor buggers out there were thin.'

'You sound like a red.'

'Me? Good God, no. I'm for trade, you know that. And old-fashioned self-interest. This thing is over, this Slump. Well, as good as. I give it about a year and we'll come out the other end. Then we can all put some beef on. But of course what we need is

65

people who've got their eyes facing front, not looking out holes in the back of their heads.'

'Practising, Ollie?'

He laughed. 'Just oiling up the vocal chords. Forgive me, Sam. That was an interesting day, out there. It gave me quite a shake-up.'

He had gone to the Akatarawa camp with a group of local government councillors, and I had tagged along to see the place. It was summer so we had dust not mud. The relief workers called the camp Aka Aka. They lived in constructions of canvas and corrugated iron, part hut, part tent, and worked building a road into the hills towards the coast — you can get the details and the colour from the piece I wrote (as much as I was able to put in). One cheeky fellow, pegging out his socks on a rope between tents, worked Ollie Joll and me aside and told us the camp had been cleaned up for our visit. 'We have our bath in the drains and wash our clothes in the horse trough. If either of you gents can wangle me a job in town? I can turn my hand to most things —' and so on.

Ollie gave him half a crown.

'I wouldn't make too much of that drains and horse-trough stuff,' he said as we caught up with our party. 'Or trust that chap as far as I can throw him.'

When we reached Lambton Quay, he said, 'Are you busy, Sam? Walk with me a little way. I'll show you a bit of the underside the Mayor and his sidekicks pretend not to see.'

We went through to the quays and moved along at an ambling pace. An easy man, perhaps a lazy man, Ollie Joll, but capable of bursts of energy generated by ambition, and by his liberal nature too. He was selfish and unselfish both, accumulating good things for himself while spreading good cheer bountifully — that's one of

66

a number of summings-up I'd attempted since Joll barged on to Council half a dozen years earlier, and one I hold to, although I've made harsher judgements recently.

After a while he said, 'Do you have any influence with James?'

'None at all.'

'What does he think he's doing, Sam? He served a useful spell, we admire him for that. But he's had his day. Can't he recognise it? You know what they'll label him? Prehistoric. He can only damage himself, coming back.'

I agreed, but wasn't going to say so. We walked some more, Joll more energetic now, agitated.

'Don't think it's self-interest making me say this. It isn't, you know, because I'll beat him, nothing surer. But it doesn't do the party any good to have us scrapping. We should be aiming all our shots at Labour now. They could win this election. They'll win the Melling seat if James is standing. But not me. I can beat them. Because I can talk to workmen, Sam, and persuade enough of them. You must see that. I've got the lingo.'

Once more, I agreed.

'And if it gets out that he's flirting with this New Zealand Legion mob, he'll do the party some real damage. We've got to keep away from that sort of stuff.'

'Who says he is? I haven't heard it.'

'He thinks the same as those people on a lot of things. And he's had a couple of meetings with Campbell Begg. Had him out for lunch at his house last week.'

'So you've got spies?'

'No, I hear things. It's something I'm good at. And one of the reasons I'll be good in Parliament. People come to me.'

Had he told me that he would let the story get out, or perhaps get in to where his party bosses kept their accounts? Either way

James was done for. I could not believe he'd been stupid enough to be seen with Begg — although he was stupid enough to share a good many of his ideas. Begg was, speaking bluntly, a loony, and his New Zealand Legion an embryo fascist party. I had had it in mind when nutting out our detective story — pushed it into deeper lunacies, of course, down where Mosley and his British fascists worked, and then a little deeper into political murder, where Campbell Begg, although a silly man, would never go. But taking even a single step with him would ruin James.

'So you hope I'm going to warn him to stay away?'

'Would you, Sam? Say you've caught a whiff.'

I shrugged, was non-committal, and wanted to get off the subject of James. I had a sense of betraying him.

'I turn off here.'

'It's only another step. Come along.'

Joll manufactured boxes, cartons, packaging of all sorts, for soap and prunes and processed cheese and Rinso, everything. He had factories in Petone and Palmerston North but kept his office upstairs from the small original one at the bottom of Taranaki Street, between Courtenay Place and the harbour. The showy man in politics became the plain businessman there.

He took me up wooden stairs, sat me in a chair in front of his desk, which was ink-stained and chipped along the edges.

'A whisky, Sam.'

'Too early for me.' My mind was still turning on James, on his obsession. He would empty all the life left to him to satisfy it.

Joll sat down. 'What I've told you, Sam, do I have to say . . . ?'

'I'll keep quiet. I'm not really a newspaperman any more. Not the newshound sort anyway. If I was, I'd wonder about you, Ollie. Why you've decided to leave Council when another term would set you right for Mayor.'

'I like a larger stage. I want to go where the big important things get done.'

'Sit on the backbench? Can you do that?'

'For a while. Not too long.' He grinned. 'And it won't be.'

'And then I'd wonder about your contradictions.'

'What do you mean?' he said, a little sharp.

'You do the large thing well, but here you are in a poky office in a run-down factory. It looks as if you can't be bothered.'

He spread his hands, then dismissed his surroundings with a flick. 'Well, I can't, Sam. Not with this. I don't spend much time here anyway. My business is sound. It's going to grow when this country gets on its feet again. In the meantime it ticks along. But it bores me, that's the truth. So I hire good people to run it. I'll go and do something more important somewhere else.'

'Your wife might have enjoyed being Mayoress,' I said, indicating the photo on his desk — a pleasant-looking woman with two shy daughters. 'The other sort of politics can be hard on families.'

'They're behind me. Dorothy knows what's what.' He frowned, his first sign of impatience. 'Anyhow, I've said my piece. I'll show you this thing I brought you for.'

The main window of the office opened above the street. A smaller one in the side wall faced the harbour, overlooking half an acre of wasteland. There, amongst mounds of trodden dirt and dried-out puddles, thirty or forty men stood in a group, staring down as though at fighting dogs or someone run over by a car. The distant cries I'd heard since climbing Joll's stairs came from there.

'What is it? Union meeting?' I said, although it seemed unlikely. Most of the men wore workmen's clothes but others were in suits like office clerks.

'They're there every day. I went out once. Won a bob,' Ollie said. 'Two Up?'

'It's harmless. It's just fun. Nobody loses much.'

'Some of them look as if they couldn't afford to.'

'Well, free men, that's what we are. There's the lookout, see, watching for the law. This is a well-organised school. They rig up poles on boxes and make a square. If you want to play, you've got to sit down.'

'And you did?' I was astonished he'd taken the risk. 'You'd end up in court. You could say goodbye to politics after that.'

'The whole of life's a risk, Sam. See how they're using dice, not pennies. Spots for heads and squares for tails.' He wanted to go down and join in.

'You're going to find Parliament pretty dull, Ollie.'

'I'll liven it up.'

A shrill whistle sounded. I mistook it for brakes squealing in the street, then saw the lookout sprinting over the waste ground towards an alley on the other side. He skidded, sending up dust, as four policemen ran from the opening in single file.

'Now this'll be good,' Ollie said.

Two cars sped up, so close their bumpers seemed locked. They braked like limousines in a movie, but constables not gangsters tumbled out. The action was furious after that — run, swerve, tackle, wriggle free; torn jacket, spinning helmet, tangle of wrestlers inside the poles as though in a ring. Men and women cheered from upstairs windows. I kept my eye on a fellow dancing like a rooster. He eluded outstretched hands with a dip and twist, hopped over fallen men, arms spread like wings, then ran free, grinning back, below our window, and slipped round into Taranaki Street. Ollie strode across the room, rattled open the front-facing window. I joined him in time to see the man dart into the factory door, leaving his hat spinning on the footpath. A chasing constable appeared, ran a little way, looked across the street.

'Yes,' Ollie called, 'over there. He went into Courtenay Place.'

'Ollie, you can't do that.'

'He's one of mine. It's not as if it's murder, Sam. Life's a game.'

The constable turned back. He picked up the hat, looked inside it for a name, then dropped it, drop-kicked it, finding none.

We watched a while longer. The police arrested ten or twelve men. The Black Maria arrived and they mounted, scowling most of them, one or two raising grazed arms, showing their wounds. The crowd clapped in the street. The doors clanged shut.

'The triumph of law and order,' Ollie said. 'Come on down, Sam. I'd better have a word with young Lennie.'

We went downstairs into the storage shed, past bales of uncut cardboard and folded sacks.

'All clear, Lennie. Out you come, boy,' Ollie said.

The man emerged from between the wall and a pile of cartons.

'How many did they get?'

'All the bosses. That's the end of that school. I wouldn't go hunting for a new one, either. If you get in court, I'll have to fire you.'

'Sure. That's fair. Can't fire yourself though, can you?'

'Don't be cheeky,' Ollie said sharply. 'And you'd better nip outside and pick up your hat before it gets pinched.'

'Sure, boss,' Lennie said, imitating some gangster from the talkies. I did not like the look of him: mouth too mobile, over-expressive, turning into a smile that might be a sneer.

'I've seen him,' I said when he had gone.

'Have you?'

'Akatarawa. He's the one who told us about the horse trough.'

'You've got a good memory, Sam.'

'So you hired him?'

71

'He got my name. Came in here. I use him as a runner. Messenger boy. He's all right. He knows the way from here to Petone and back. Saves me some work.'

'He looks like a smart alec,' I said.

'Sure, he is. Anyhow, Sam, if you want a story, Lennie's not the only one. I've got a file of letters up there this thick.' He showed me with his hands. 'Men wanting work. Telling me what they can do. Do you know about desperation? I'll give you some to read.'

'Everyone in politics gets letters like that. James still gets them, and he's out.'

'Yes, but they chuck them in the waste-paper bin. I do something. I find jobs. I try, at least. Does James do that? I must have found fifteen or twenty men jobs.'

Lennie came back with his hat.

'I was two bob up out there,' he said.

'Hard luck. Go and see Jean. There's a pile of stuff for Petone.'

'Can I take the car?'

'No, the train. Go on, shift. Earn your pay.'

'Sure, boss.'

I shook hands with Ollie and walked home along the harbour front. Lennie passed me, sprinting again, with a brown-paper parcel held like a football in his arm.

'He should pay me for that two bob I lost,' he yelled.

He was like Owen Moody: looked nineteen but was probably thirty. If he'd come to me for a job, I'd have barred the windows.

Five

That busy two or three months seems all outings. I'm a man who likes to sit at home, with a record on the gramophone: Peter Dawson, John Charles Thomas, Richard Tauber. I like sea shanties, plain emotions, love of the countryside and the sea, of women and of being in love. I like robustness and a soaring voice, no tremolo, after my life of hunting among grubby successes and faked emotions and greedy schemes for this bit of news and that. It's a second-rate life. I like to sit with Tennyson, Rudyard Kipling, John Masefield, Alfred Noyes, only Rose in the room with me, reading too, and find beauty in that company, and fresh clean thought. Then my home is 'bright with a calm delight', in the words of another poet. But March, April, May, I seemed to be always in galleries and halls and meeting rooms and in our city's 'pent streets'.

Eric was a man for being out and about — lectures, concerts, meetings, wrestling matches: he went to them all, dragging me along when he could. We walked up Lambton Quay, took the cable car to Upland Road, enjoyed the view over the harbour to the black elephantine hills beyond Days Bay, enjoyed the moon, Eric with his scientist's eye, I with my poet manqué's (he explained the craters, I replied with young Robin Hyde's 'the scornful crystal moon'), then walked along the crest of the hill to the observatory, where he gave a talk on Jupiter and its satellites, showing slides of them on a screen.

When we came out, a woman from the audience stood waiting in the forecourt, her clothes moon-silvered on one side, gilded on the other by light flooding from the door.

'Professor Clifton, that was most enjoyable. I think my favourite is Ganymede.'

Eric introduced us. She was Mrs Maxey, a small, well-rounded woman of sixty or so, with a considering eye but, as far as I could tell, a comfortable nature. She wore a modest boa, no fox face peeping out, and a grey dress with a silky shine. Her car was parked in Upland Road. Could she offer us a lift?

'We'll walk you there,' Eric said. 'But Sam and I are going down through the cemetery. We're meeting our wives.'

Mrs Maxey laughed and Eric, waking up, laughed too: 'No, no, they're alive and well. We're meeting them at Parliament.'

I wondered at the hint of flirtatiousness between him and this woman, and his countervailing defensiveness. He had been quick to mention wives. We went past the cable car terminus, talking of moons — Jupiter's multitude and our one — and disputing light-heartedly (I was silent) about the naming of more, should they appear. At the car, she said, 'Our new moons will be Savage and Fraser, don't you think?'

'Heaven forbid. No politics up there. The Germans would want Hitler and the Russians Stalin. I'd sooner name them One, Two and Three. But I know what you mean, Savage and Co. Their time is right, and a good thing too.'

She looked at him archly. 'In spite of all the experience on the other side.'

'Ha!' he said. He opened her car door, handed her in and she drove away.

'I've seen her somewhere,' I said.

'I hope not.'

'Why?'

He was quiet for a moment, but had let himself in for telling me. We walked into the park. 'She's the owner of a little brothel over by the Basin Reserve. It's very select. Discreet, you know? You can't go unless you're recommended. That makes for a small clientele.' He laughed. 'I like the idea of Mrs Maxey blackballing certain people.'

I said nothing.

'You're not shocked, Sam?'

'What's a woman like that doing at a talk on astronomy?'

'Come off it. Do you think a brothel keeper can't have a mental life? She comes to lots of my talks. She's got books over there even you haven't read. It's planetology, by the way.'

'So you've been?'

'You're pretty sharp. Moralists can see the tiniest crack. But rest easy, boy. I only make social calls. It's in the same building, but she keeps a firewall between.'

He seemed too glib — and I had got a sniff of more than acquaintanceship between them. He saw the look I gave: believing only half, demanding more.

'I've been friends with her for fifty years. She was in my class at primary school. And later on she was my girlfriend for a while. She was my first. I mean that I ever made love to. And very nice too. Amazing in fact. Like finding a new comet. You don't forget those things. Oh come on, Sam, get that look off your face.'

'Were you her first?'

'You wouldn't ask a question like that about a respectable lady. The answer's no. She had a liking for it, an aptitude. She's honest, Sam. No humbug. I've said enough. If you don't want to walk with me, say so. I'll turn off here.'

77

'How do you know her these days, when you're married?'

'I go and visit her. We talk about all sorts of things. Do you think some sort of moral pollution comes through the walls?'

'Does May know you go there?'

'I might knock you down in the gutter soon.'

'Does she?'

'No. Now shut up. You're starting to remind me of James.'

We went past Seddon's grandiose memorial, past Harry Holland's, gleaming white and showing too much buttock for my taste. I understood Mrs Maxey's remark about Ganymede and felt a burning in my throat — had to spit. Anything but clean love — married love — between a man and a woman denies our humanity: I mean our status as creation's recipient of a sense of right and good. I won't go on. It has nothing to do with church religion, which Rose and I scarcely practise anyhow.

Eric and I walked down the paths by 'the dreaming graves' and I grew calmer. He came some way to meet me after a while: 'Have you heard of albedo?'

'Something to do with light?'

'The amount that gets reflected from a planet or a moon. Well, May reflects like Venus. That's seventy per cent coming back. She keeps the rest. But with Lily Maxey almost nothing comes. It's like Mercury, fourteen per cent. You understand that? She clever and she's friendly but she sucks up light. Not her fault, it's the way she is.'

'Why do you go, then?'

'Friendship, mainly. She'd be offended. All right, a little bit of excitement too. Not her any more, the girls through the wall. Can't help thinking about it, Sam. But I don't cross over. Ah, you're going to spit again. Don't say you don't feel it sometimes. All the pretty girls in the street?'

'No, I don't. I don't want to listen any more.'

78

'Rightyho. But remember, May is the one with the light.'

'And the other one is Mercury. You know what they used that for.'

Eric laughed. I had not meant it as a joke but it pleased him enormously. My bit of science, I suppose.

We walked down to Bowen Street, past the Alexander Turnbull Library, where old Johannes Andersen guards the books, and round to the front of Parliament. There was King Dick again, not mourned by Robed State now but belly out, arm upraised, dissembling in his own honest way. The three yellow lamps signalled that the House was sitting.

We went through the corridors and met the *Dominion* reporter coming out.

'Hello, Sam. There's fireworks. The ladies are out in force. The Old Boys are looking hag-ridden.'

'Who's up now?'

'Walter Nash. Time for me to have a smoke.'

I could have gone into the Press Gallery. It would have got me away from Eric, whom I wanted to be distant from for a while, but that would mean explaining to Rose and I did not want the subject raised with her. I followed him into the Strangers. There was no room on the benches so we stood at the back. Over in the Women's Gallery, Rose and May had seats among a group of women I took for housewives and working women — cleaners, shop assistants and the like. They leaned forward, all of them, as though to take a bite — although with Nash speaking it was more likely to get a breath of his socialist air.

He gravelled and tack-spat through his time, thumped the desk, making water jump from his glass.

'He's on form,' Eric said.

'I've heard too much ranting in my time.'

Nash sat down to cries of Hear, hear, good on you, Walter, from the women, and one or two men around us too. The debate was on unemployment. It roused strong passions, which surfaced as anger when Bodkin rose for the Government. He was a droning speaker. The tactic was to kill the argument with platitudes. 'If you increase the relief pay, that raises the associated issue of a rise in un-employment tax.'

'Put up the tax of the people who've got all the loot. You can call it the fatties' tax,' cried the woman sitting next to May — a big-boned creature with rolled-up sleeves and meaty forearms and a red washerwoman's face. An orderly pounced on her and although she looked as if she could have picked him up by the britches and dropped him over the rail she allowed him to lead her out.

Bodkin started again but the shouters were primed for him, sitting not in a block but here and there, in both galleries, so the orderlies would not know where the next interjection would come from.

'Women and children are starving in Wellington and this man spouts about shillings and pence. You should be damned well drowned on those benches.' Out she went.

'We'll get what we want, wait and see. We'll damned well take it.' He followed.

The Speaker heard threat as well as noise and adjourned the sitting. People crowded the rails as the members filed out. May leaned too, calling abuse. Rose sat still, my steady wife.

'It's bread for our children we're asking for. Give us that.'

'Hae you niver thought you hae your God to meet? You hae your maker? You'll nae escape frae him.'

I frowned at the silliness — that hunger, anger, pain should take such form. But Eric had a flushed face and a lively eye, and if there had been a place at the rail would have shouted too.

We met our wives by Dick Seddon's statue.

'Blatherers. Liars,' May said. She looked as if she might tear her clothes.

'Both sides, May?' Eric said, cooler now.

She looked at him scornfully. 'They need their watches and waistcoats stripped off. And someone to put them out in the bush digging a road. With their wives and children living off turnips at home.'

'You should have said so. I was waiting for you.'

'Those women have earned their right to speak. I haven't.'

He had his car parked in Molesworth Street, but I told him Rose and I would walk, enjoy the night — which turned out not to be a lie. It had an autumn smell and laid warm air on our cheeks. We did not talk about the scenes in Parliament. Rose knew I did not like her getting involved; and I that she would not apologise. She took my arm.

All I allowed myself was to say at the gate: 'May makes too much noise for me.'

'Me too, sometimes. The trouble is, she's usually right.'

I said nothing about Eric.

In May he gave the Donovan Lecture in the Concert Chamber. I had heard him there in 1931, when he talked about the moon and how new studies, in which he had been prominent, building on the work of Bickerton and Gifford, had proved that its craters were formed by meteor impact and not by volcanic activity, as had been thought. He thrilled us that night as much with his eminence, his role in world science, as with the moon itself.

'Looking back to a period soon after the birth of the solar system,' he began, 'we see the Earth and moon as glowing masses of rotating vapour or of molten metals in a fiery liquid state.'

He had me at once. Yes, I cried, with full conviction, knowing nothing. I sat entranced as he rolled on, demonstrating truth by his voice and presence.

'In the case of the Earth nearly all the speed of a meteorite is destroyed while it passes through the air. On the moon, however, every meteorite strikes with its full velocity.'

Eric, too, struck at full speed. I was first on to my feet in the standing ovation he received.

On the night of his Donovan Lecture I was less carried away. He warned that we must pay close attention; that the huge drama being enacted in the depths of space, thousands of light years away, which we might imagine as a contest between suns, came down in his studies, and those of his peers (and he was not a leader, he emphasised), to the severe and formal working out of celestial mechanics. He talked about Novae and Double and Variable stars, explaining them in ways that his audience could — but only just — understand.

I sat in the front row with Rose and May and James and Vi and Charlie. Other things were on my mind. Politics at that time seemed more important than stars. The local body elections had just been held, generating a heat that would last, and steadily grow, until the national ones at the end of the year. Hislop had beaten Semple for the Wellington mayoralty and Citizens 9 had beaten Labour 6 for Council. Charlie reported that James had said (not cried), 'Hooray.' As for Dunedin, where Labour had taken control: 'It's nothing,' he declared. 'A sore big toe. We'll soon put a bandage on that.' He must have been feeling good to joke.

And only a day or two before, the Reform and United Parties had announced their amalgamation — resisting, they said, the imminent challenge of the alien doctrines of socialism.

Strange that two mortal enemies should join, but too late to stem the rising tide, Savage retorted.

'Red, tide, red tide,' James said. 'They'll bleed the country dry, suck out the blood' — getting himself in soapbox mode, worrying about his language less.

But still he had not said that he would go for the nomination. Joll was making it no secret that he would try. The selection meeting was only three weeks away.

'I won't let some Johnny-come-lately set my timetable,' James said.

He seemed calm. Yet an inner tension worked in him. Forces met, pushing in opposite ways. One looked for hairline fractures in his face. Perhaps this is hindsight — or perhaps a consequence of the porcelain mask Charlie had painted on him in her picture. I could not forget.

Vi gave a little moan beside me. 'I don't understand what he's talking about.'

'It's over soon. Just a few more minutes.'

She alarmed me. The last time I had seen her I had thought her ill with frustrated selfishness. Now she seemed threatened by something outside herself, as if she had poked some sleeping creature with a stick and it had risen to its feet and was looking at her. Vi was afraid. Her cheeks were hollowed, with a bluish tinge; her bones were showing. One expected, if one listened, as with James, to hear the crackle of tiny fractures taking place inside.

He should not have brought her to the lecture but must have thought the time was right to have her at his side: James Tinling and his wife on show.

Oliver Joll sat two rows behind with Mrs Joll, who seemed to understand what Eric was talking about. Joll laughed at his jokes — no matter what the subject, Eric would have one or two — and spread his presence around him like the odour of manliness and success.

Eric crescendoed. He can be phoney at times. Applause burst like a continuation.

We made our way to the foyer, where Freddie and Elsie latched on to us.

'Oh, he's too clever,' Elsie cried. 'I believe he just pretends that stuff.'

'How can he know, if everything's so far away?' Freddie said.

There's never any need to answer them. James, with his hand locking Vi's on his forearm, moved aside to talk to Dunning, a member of the committee that would choose the new party's Melling candidate. (Reform, United, what would the party name itself, and would it formalise its union or keep it only for the election?) I expected Joll too would have Dunning in his sights, but he seemed content with nonentities. Beyond him, Mrs Maxey, the brothel woman, settled her thin fur about her shoulders and went alone into the night.

'Sam,' Joll said, stepping close, 'Clifton's your brother-in-law, isn't he? I'd like to meet him.'

'He should be here in a moment,' I said. 'This is Mrs Clifton.' I introduced Rose as well, and, perforce, Elsie and Freddie. Charlie had moved away to speak with the painter Frank Siers, her teacher before she left New Zealand. Joll beckoned his wife and we made an uneasy group, exclaiming at Eric's brilliance and talking platitudes. I noticed Taylor Barr and Owen Moody edging close, but turned my shoulder; after a moment they drifted off, Moody looking resentful, which pleased me. He had not earned his right to force his way into conversations.

'Eric,' I said, when he steamed up, 'I'd like you to meet Mr and Mrs Joll. Oliver Joll.'

We told him how brilliantly he had talked — no exaggeration. Eric performs like a showman, dragging his audience along, keeping them on a forward slant and breathless at the mystery about to be revealed. He's Houdini playing tricks with chains and padlocks, and Faraday laying down new facts for all to see.

'It's not an easy subject,' Joll said, 'but I think I grasp some of it now. But how can we — humans, I mean, tiny specks of matter in the universe — how can we translate those distances and speeds into words and figures we can understand? Put them on a human scale?'

'By visceral means,' Eric boomed. 'If you try to send your understanding out, you'll get nowhere. Send out your eye, send out your heartbeat if you like, then you'll get an image coming back, and you might hear the throb of the universe too.'

He was drunk with completion. Any old words would do him now.

Rose and I were putting on a supper and I made signs that we should move on. Mrs Joll had taken issue with her husband's 'specks of matter':

'We're animated by spirit, surely, even if we don't believe in souls.'

'Spirit is continuous,' Eric cried. 'Perhaps we'll travel through space in that way. Instantaneously.' He seemed to hear himself and grinned shamefacedly. 'A drop of the other sort of spirits would go down.'

'Yes, we'll make a move,' I said.

Joll drew me aside. 'Sam, do you know what James is doing yet?'

'Playing cagey. Don't ask me. It's three weeks, Ollie. You can hang on.'

'Can he?'

'What do you mean?'

'He doesn't look well. Is that his wife? Nor does she.'

He was out of order, and recognised it, yet could not prevent himself from saying, 'I wish I knew what game he's playing.' He was less of a politician than I'd thought; should not have let me see his worry. I patted his arm and told him I had enjoyed meeting his wife.

'And I'm delighted to meet the Professor,' he said. 'That's a privilege. It's remarkable the people he attracts.' He was nodding at Taylor and Owen Moody, who, I saw, had broken into James's talk with his committee man. Yet the pair looked at ease, while James was wearing one of his less wintry smiles.

'The one who's grinning is my nephew. The other's a hanger-on.'

'I think I've seen him.'

'Owen Moody. Aspires to be a poet.'

'Ha!' Ollie said. 'Well, we'll let you get away. A fascinating evening, Sam.'

I drove home and put the car in the garage while Rose ran inside to turn on the lights and take the muslin cloths off the food she had prepared. Eric and May arrived, bringing Elsie and Freddie; and there, puttering on his motorcycle, playing obedient son, was Taylor Barr, with Owen Moody, goggled and leather-coated, on the pillion seat. I felt a squirt of rage: was there no way to be rid of the fellow?

He smiled like George Formby: 'I won't eat much, Mr Holloway.'

'Where's James?' I said to Eric.

'Coming along. I told Charlie she could bring her painter friend. They're planning an exhibition.'

'The more the merrier,' I said sourly.

The painter, Siers, was a florid fellow — whisky cheeks, veined nose, snow-white hair; florid in his speech too, full of loose adjectives. It was as well he made a lot of noise, for Eric seemed to have run out of steam and we stood without a centre. Rose had taken Vi to a bedroom to lie down. James sat in my chair, sipping tea. May, smiling privately, moved close to Eric and leaned on him, privately too, and it seemed amorously, which was misplaced for the occasion. Handing him beer, I could smell him: sweaty from the work of lecturing.

I made a little speech, thanking Eric for an informative and stimulating evening, then proposed a toast to him.

'I'm out of words,' he replied. 'The stars are out there still, shall we go and look?'

The street lights and house lights were too strong and we were half-hearted, so we trooped back inside, where James, who had not shifted from his chair, said, 'See if your mother's ready, Girl. I'd like to go.'

Charlie went to the bedroom, and in a moment Rose came out and beckoned May.

Siers, the painter, saw his chance. 'Mr Tinling,' he said, 'Charlotte and I are planning an exhibition together. It will be in my studio. Pupil and teacher — we'll see a line of continuity perhaps. The torch handed on. Although she's emerging, the butterfly breaks from the chrysalis. Those Parisians she's been following will turn out not to be important now she's home. She's seeing our light again, our glorious light. And yet holding literal truth at arm's length, in her way. Her vision is remarkably pure, don't you think?' He laughed. 'And mine's not bad. What I'd like to ask — I'd be honoured if you would open it.'

'I know nothing about art,' James said. 'I can't oblige. Taylor, will you tell my man to bring the car. He's parked along the street somewhere.'

'Mr Tinling,' Siers said, 'your own daughter —'

'I don't see eye to eye with Charlotte about her painting. You'll have to get someone else.' He stubbed out his cigarette and stood up. 'Thank you for a pleasant evening, Sam. Eric, you too. An interesting subject. Are the women ready yet?'

They were not. Rose came in. 'James, Vi is going to stay the night. I've put her in bed. She's —' saw the listeners — 'feeling a wee bit off colour. Do you want to go in and see her?'

James made no word — made a twitch of annoyance, which he disguised.

'If she's in bed it's better not to disturb her. I'll call tomorrow. It's nothing new, I hope?'

'She's just over-tired. We'll keep her here a few days, if that's all right. That will give Charlie a rest too.'

'Where's she?'

'Coming soon. She's saying goodnight.'

James sat down. 'When she's ready,' he said.

'Mr Tinling,' Siers began, but I shepherded him away: 'Not now.' I wanted him out of the house — everyone out.

He saw my mood and went for his coat. I walked down the path with him.

'Extraordinary. What's wrong with the man?' he said.

'Goodnight, Mr Siers.'

He stumped away as James's car came along the street and stopped at my gate. I heard laughter from inside: heard the driver's door open and saw a face rise above the hood, illumined by the street lamp. Fag in mouth, hat pushed back, teeth a-grin.

'Gidday,' he said.

It was a surprise too many. My world tilted, throwing me sideways.

'What are you doing here?'

'My new job. I'm a shoffer.' It was the boy/man Lennie, Oliver Joll's messenger.

'You work for Joll.'

'Not any more. I quit. It's better wages. And a motor of me own'. A sentence broken cleverly: toff the first part, street-corner lout the second.

Taylor, climbing out the passenger door, laughed.

'Do you know this person?' I demanded.

88

'Just met him,' Taylor said. 'What's wrong, Unc?'

'He works for Joll. Does Mr Tinling know?' I said to Lennie.

'I left Joll's.'

'But I bet you report back to him.'

Owen Moody had climbed from the back seat. 'I don't think you can accuse him without any evidence.'

'Do you know him?'

'Like Taylor, we just met.'

'I'd smoked all my fags so I cadged one,' Lennie said.

'What's your second name?'

'Ferrabee. Len Ferrabee. I showed him references, all that.'

'One from Joll?'

'Never got one. I walked out. Couldn't take any more of that big boss stuff.'

'Give him a break, Uncle. He'll lose his job if you tell on him,' Taylor said.

The coincidence was too great. I was sure the fellow was a spy — yet a careless one, to let himself be discovered so easily.

Owen Moody said, 'This would make a good bit for our novel. Conspiracies, eh?'

'If Joll and James are after the same seat,' I began — but these were not the people I should be talking to.

I started for the house. Charlie and James came on to the porch.

'James, your driver used to work for Joll,' I said.

'Yes,' James said, adjusting his scarf, 'he told me. He doesn't like the fellow any more than I do. Goodnight, Sam.'

Lennie Ferrabee grinned from the street and raised his hat. Taylor laughed, while Moody hid a smile. Charlie kissed me.

'He drives nice and slow. You've got to for Da.' She seemed relaxed, perhaps from talking with a fellow artist; would not know of James's refusal yet, had probably not known that Siers would ask or she'd have stopped him.

Owen Moody held the car door open. Ferrabee flicked his cigarette butt over the hood on to my lawn. He climbed in, engaged the gears, drove smoothly away. Owen and Taylor came back to the house for their coats. I did not want to speak to them, so crossed the lawn and ground out Ferrabee's butt with my heel. What was going on? James knew the man had worked for Joll. Was it James who was running a spy? Impossible. The whole thing had to be a coincidence. Except that Ferrabee was the smart-alec type James would never employ.

All my remaining guests were on the path: Eric and May, Elsie and Freddie, Taylor and Moody.

'Skulking, Sam?' Eric said.

'Hooligans,' I said, picking up the cigarette butt and throwing it into the street.

I saw them off and went inside.

'How long is she staying?' I said to Rose. I felt a desperate need for simplicity. I wanted to be alone with my wife.

'Don't start, Sam. It's not her fault.'

'She chose her life.'

'Not now, please. I'll have to sit with her for a while. Do you want to go in and say goodnight?'

'No, I don't.'

'Go and get some sleep then. You'll feel better in the morning.'

I went to my study instead and poured another drink. Soon I began to feel ashamed. I could look in to where Rose sat and say I was sorry, but that might mean speaking with Vi as well; so I fetched a tray from the kitchen and cleared away the dirty dishes and uneaten food.

Rose opened the door and whispered, 'Thanks,' as I went to bed.

Vi would have stayed all winter, but Rose and May between them persuaded her that better care and comfort lay at home. James had said he might hire a nurse. Charlie came to fetch her in the car with Ferrabee. She promised she would stop James putting Vi on show again — but James, I'm sure, had made that decision for himself.

I went inside, breathed deeply. The woman was gone. My house felt spacious and clean aired. I resolved to stay put, and when I went out to keep my eyes front and not engage with things that did not concern me. Rose sat beside me on the sofa. I put my arm around her and we stayed quiet and still. She was grieving for her sister's broken life and I allowed myself to feel a little sadness too.

We worked in the garden in the afternoon. How still the day was, how sufficient this place and company.

Then events began to move again, and people reached out and put their hands on me.

Six

The selection meeting. I was not there but see it in my mind's eye like an ill-shot movie, jumping gaps from frame to frame. Here's Joll, here's James, speaking, smiling, raising dramatic palm, then facing each other with made-up faces, white and still. Each will be the hero. Only one can be. It is Joll. His face grows dark with triumph and his smile expands. He flickers suddenly as things speed up — faces the hundred faces, raising his arms over his head like a boxer, while James, wearing a thin smile, nods his head once and steps up and shakes Joll firmly by the hand. Joll wants to hang on, make it matey, but James disengages and his black-coated back goes out the door. His white gloves flash. His top hat gleams. He is gone. Joll stands alone with his victory.

Top hat? Gloves? What stuff I make up — yet it's not invented, it's what I see. And I see James reach home and sit in his study in the dark as the hall clock strikes one, two, three. He smokes a cigarette and stares between heavy folds of curtain at the night.

I did not travel out to the Hutt Valley but called him on the telephone to commiserate — and found him spry voiced, talkative. I thought, Well, the obsession's gone, the weight has lifted. James

95

can be a free man again. No more sleepless nights, no more looking into the dark.

'I see why they chose him. They're wrong of course,' he said. 'But as you pointed out, Sam, there are tides that flow in politics and it does no good opposing them. The better man lost, but that's no unusual event. How are you and Rose? Oh, and thank you for looking after Violet so well. I think she'll turn the corner soon. Charlotte says she's eating more.'

I risked re-introducing Joll.

James made a sound of contempt. 'At least he'll beat the Labour fellow. I suppose that's to the good. Whether he's got the intelligence ... It's noise isn't it, most of the time, and striking poses? Well, this is the age of the vulgarian. Let's not talk about him. Do you see where Lawrence of Arabia's dead? What a sad thing. These motorcycles. We must make sure that Taylor rides carefully —' and so on. John Buchan — more importantly, Baron Tweedsmuir — appointed Governor-General of Canada. 'We could do with that sort of chap out here.'

I hung up with relief — and was relieved for him.

Eric had the same conversation. In spite of the chatter, it made him think that James had suddenly grown old. We agreed that life might be easier now — James pottering in his roses and taking up bowls instead of tennis. The court would make a good croquet green.

'I'd like to try that game,' Eric said wistfully. He took me to the wrestling instead, where Lofty Blomfield used his Indian Death Lock on Ken Kenneth.

The next night our novel-writing group met to hear Owen Moody read his chapter. Nine of our original twelve were left. Marcus Waller was gone, Tom Gow was gone — his letter was pompous and ill phrased; I was pleased to be rid of him — and, sadly, Roy Kember had sunk almost overnight into a slough of despond and feebleness. All his lost ambition, wasted chances, dragged him down. It is not part of my story, his despair and dotage, so I'll leave it.

Roy was my friend.

'I'll write an extra chapter if you like. I'll do Tom Gow's. Put in some pleats,' Owen Moody said.

This boy is hard of heart, I thought. He's a *je m'en fiche-ist*. 'You're still on probation. Let's hear your own chapter,' I said.

We were in my study, crammed in, wreathed in smoke and, I supposed, mellowed by our first glasses of beer.

'Point of order,' Euan Poynter said. 'I'd like to think that just because we're dabbling in murder we don't have to let our standards drop. No criticism intended, but there seems to be a falling away. We all like our pint, and no one takes too much, but — hmm, nothing personal — anyone looking in might think we're a bit of a rabble. Not quite the clean potato, don't you think?'

I told him I did not follow.

Owen Moody gave a laugh, almost a shout. 'He means me. My cravat. I don't believe this.'

'Is that it, Euan? You think he should wear a tie?'

'It's just, well, how we feel about our status. Senior writers and all that. I know we have to let some young ones in, and move over gracefully, so to speak, but nevertheless, standards, you know. I'll say no more.'

'Does anyone agree with Euan?' I asked. No one did. 'Then we'll get on.'

But I saw the tightness in Euan Poynter's face. He had expected to win his point by seniority, urbanity and what he thought of as his common touch. Another one lost, I thought. We're falling apart.

'I've got some flasher ones than this,' Owen Moody said, flicking his cravat free from his jacket. 'I'll wear one next time.'

'Let's leave it,' I said, 'leave it alone. More beer, anyone? Top up your glasses. All right, Owen. Read what you've got. Just remember where we are —' I looked around. 'Jennifer Woodley has been kidnapped. And our journalist hero, Rufus Worthington — is there anyone here like me who doesn't think that name's quite right? No? We'll discuss it later. Rufus has found the house by the Basin Reserve. He's investigating, creeping up the stairs, when someone on the landing whacks him on the head with a blackjack. Lights out. Carry on, Owen.'

' "Chapter eight",' Owen read, his voice changing in a way that startled us: authority. ' "He could not tell if sound or movement caused his agony. A thin whining cut him like a knife — a blade sliding into his eye socket, into the space where memory of who and why and where must lie. With it came a vibration, and a backward pressure that meant — his first coherent thought — forward motion. The jolt of a pot-hole, a sideways tilt, a lurch of gears: he was in a car, blindfolded, hands and feet tied. A voice above and forward of him grunted, 'How's our pretty boy in the back?'

' "In spite of his pain and fear, Rufus was instantly alert. He knew who he was and where he was, but not who with, or why, and knew himself to be in mortal danger ..." '

Owen read on. The thug in the passenger seat, his eyebrows meeting (Owen's joke: he would take it out, he told us later — and anyway, how would Rufus see if he was blindfolded?) — the thug reaches back and slaps Rufus casually on the mouth. 'Leave him,' the driver says, in an educated voice.

I have a copy with me as I write — need it for quotation, but not for impact, which can never be repeated. I remember thinking: This boy is the goods.

The car climbs a hill, changing down, coughing in its throat. A gate squeaks open, a garage door groans. The educated voice says, 'Bring him.'

Inside a house he is forced on to his knees. 'Tell us how you found us.' They slap and punch him, then burn him with a cigarette. ('No!' Euan Poynter exclaimed. No one else agreed.) Rufus howls inside himself but does not say a word. They untie his hands to break his fingers. ('No!': Euan Poynter.) But Rufus cries, 'Where's Jennifer? What have you done with her?' The educated man laughs: 'I think we've caught the boyfriend. Leave his fingers, Morry. He's in enough pain from love already.' He tells Rufus that Jennifer is 'trussed up like a chicken' in the house by the Basin Reserve. 'If you'd opened one more door you would have found her. Hard luck.' He tells the thugs Rufus has been acting alone. 'Lock him in the shed. You can take him out and dump him in the morning.'

Rufus tries to see beneath the bottom of his blindfold. There are three pairs of shoes, one of them Italian. The educated man says, 'You can dream of her tonight, Algernon. That's as close as you're going to get.' The thugs guffaw. They tie his hands, drag him outside, throw him on a dirt floor in a shed.

Owen took a sip of beer. He smiled at us. Was there something contemptuous in it? Then he read on: brisk, clipped, fast, personal. I kept on thinking: He knows, he knows.

Rufus is a match for the thugs. He has read Houdini's autobiography and knows the trick of swelling his wrist muscles while the ropes are being tied. He has perhaps half an inch of play. Coolly, yet desperately for there will be no second chance, he sets to work, wondering all the time if he will be a match for the man with the educated voice.

I'll skip the rope bits — they are too long. He frees his hands, takes off his blindfold. When his eyes can see, he makes out high walls, a high window, a half-attic for storage at the back of the shed. The moon shines in. He unties his feet, gets his circulation back. Rufus explores. The door is barred on the outside. There is no way out.

Owen wrote with sinew and blood: I mean, you knew this was a man saving himself by courage, dexterity and physical strength. Our detective story had turned to action and was alive. I think we all knew — even Eric, although he was grinning with interest — that we had been pushed aside, or rather, stood down, and had no part in our book any more.

He (Rufus) uses a plank of wood to climb to the attic. He walks on beams like a tightrope walker to the high window over the door, forces it open, wriggles through, drops to the ground. He crouches, working out what to do next. Steal the car? No, they will be on to him before he can get those groaning doors open and the engine started. He looks out to sea, where Kapiti Island rolls its whaleback on the horizon. A motor boat is anchored a hundred yards off shore. He understands 'dump him'. They will tie something heavy on him and take him out and drop him over the side. For a moment he is paralysed with fear. Then fear for Jennifer galvanises him. He must get back to the house by the Basin Reserve and rescue her before these killers find out he is gone.

He runs for the beach, crouching low.

The house door opens. A man comes out, a slighter man than the muscular thugs. He stands on the veranda, looking out to sea. Rufus lies on his stomach, peering through a bush. The man walks down the steps and starts for the beach. Rufus crouches on the sand, under a crumbling overhang. Soft footsteps sound. The man stops at the top of the bank and looks out over the ruffled sea. The moon lights his face and Rufus, peering through a fringe of grass, sees that he is young, scarcely more than a boy, with a high shining forehead and black hair, hooded eyes catching glints of light, a nose like a blade, a bitter mouth with a silver scar turning up one corner like a smile. For a moment he thinks it is a woman dressed as a man. He knows he has seen her before.

The man speaks. The spell breaks. 'I will,' he says.

We sat breathless, our pipes going cold, our forgotten glasses in our hands. Owen smiled — broke his own spell. 'Not too much?' he inquired.

'No, no. Go on.'

' "The words cut like diamonds, in that English voice, and Rufus, under the bank, on hands and knees, knew that this man would out-think him, out-fight him. "I will." A terrible will, reducing other lives to dead matchsticks, garden slugs. He lowered his eyes from the bright face.

' "How long he crouched there he did not know. The man had only to lower his eyes to discover him. He was imperious and beautiful and deadly, standing unseen yet printed forever on Rufus's memory." '

Too much, I thought; and Owen frowned, thinking so too. He coughed, read on.

The villain, the educated boy/man, woman/man, takes out a cigarette, strikes a match. He stands smoking. The breeze from the sea drops for a moment. Smoke curls down and Rufus, alert again, fighting back, identifies the Turkish smell of the cigarettes John Woodley had favoured.

After smoking for a moment, the man drops his cigarette on the sand, where it burns half an inch from Rufus's palm. He turns and walks back to the house; sees the half-open window in the shed; runs to the door, flings it open. He turns to the house and screams like a eunuch, 'Morry, Bluey, he's got away. Let the dogs loose.'

Cool again, thinking again, Rufus picks up the cigarette. He grinds out the burning tip in the sand, puts the butt in his pocket: evidence. He heads for the water in a crouching run.

I won't do all the action: Rufus swimming, bullets pocking the water by his head, two huge hounds going crazy at the water-line, a dinghy launched from the boathouse; the motorboat engine that won't start and the anchor that won't free; more bullets smashing into the hull; then the roar of the motor, the bow wave swamping the dinghy, sending Morry and Bluey into the sea; and last of all, as Rufus roars away down the moonlit coast, the villain, moonlit too, standing on the beach, his voice raised in a howl, his white scar gleaming.

We sighed. One or two clapped.

'Well done, my boy,' Theo Mead said.

'I don't like the torture. And nor do I like "eunuch",' Euan Poynter said. 'There's also the matter of sentences without verbs.'

No one took any notice of him.

'Who is he? This villain?' Eric said.

'Well,' Owen said, 'he's from my dreams. I have them where I'm hunted and I hide and there's someone coming for me but I never see his face. So I've tried to, in this . . . I can't explain.'

'No need. But what it means is we have to rewrite some stuff in the early chapters —'

'Where is it leading?' Euan Poynter cried. 'Who is this villain, do we know? He was older and bald-headed in my chapter.'

'We can fix that,' Eric said.

'He's John Woodley's illegitimate son, who's been put in an orphanage, where he got his scar. Woodley's kept him secret. But he's hunted his father down —'

'And killed him? Impossible.'

'And it makes him Jennifer's half-brother, which is why he's kidnapped her. And why Rufus thinks he knows the man: he looks like her. As for the political stuff, he's using the plotters for his private revenge.'

'We could make that woman from my chapter, the one in the glory box — she could be his mother, how about that?' Theo Mead said.

'Hold on, hold on,' I said.

'There's no going back, Sam. Not when we've got something like this,' Eric said.

'Writing like this,' Theo said.

'There was a misrelated participle,' Euan cried.

'I vote we pull out and let Owen finish it.'

'How did he get his voice, this English voice? Not in an orphanage,' I said.

'By an act of will.'

'And his money? He seems to have plenty of that.'

'Will. Will power. What he needs for his revenge, he'll get.'

'I don't know.'

'I don't think it's our story any more, Sam,' Eric said.

'I won't give up my chapter,' Euan cried.

We smoked more pipes and cigarettes and drank more beer and shifted around uneasily — several, perhaps, relieved — on the broken ground of our idea. Gave up at midnight, with nothing decided but with the knowledge that Owen Moody had picked us up and put us down in another place.

I had thought we might become famous. I had imagined laudatory reviews, an American edition, a French translation. I'd interviewed myself for the Wellington papers and held out my hand for fat royalty cheques.

Should I work out another plot and write it in secret, by myself?

Rose was asleep. I could not ask her.

I am trying to turn then into now. I'm pretending that I don't know what will happen.

There must be no over-arching consciousness. I know what Owen Moody's chapter means, but I did not know at the time. All I can say is, it delighted us while confounding us. Our arrogance, advantage in years, gone. I would have welcomed one of those woman writers along (those 'girls' we'd sidelined with such satisfaction) to cure Owen Moody's own arrogance; teach him some measure and restraint.

'I'll be in touch, Owen. There's some things we need to talk about.'

'I'm a bit busy, Sam.' I had not invited him to call me Sam. 'Can it wait?'

So to bed — but little sleep. I was haunted in my half-waking dreams by the man with the silver scar.

Several days later Euan Poynter withdrew. He complained of 'the cult of violence this young man promotes' and 'the proliferating of psychology'. For good measure, he Poynted out other people's faults, including my 'incoherent style and subfusc language'. Stewart Peebles wrote and said he had decided not to go on. Our group eroded. But I was not ready to give up. I thought Owen and I between us might complete the book. I believed I was better at plotting than him. Half the credit would be mine, even if he 'unpleated' my prose.

Seven

---

*I*n July Charlie and Frank Siers held their joint show in Siers's studio on The Terrace. Edith Lendrum, the flower painter, gave the speech. It was a brave performance: she liked what she saw, but knew the trouble she invited for saying so.

'Painting cannot always stay the same,' she said. 'Year after year we perpetuate the Victorian taste. We suffer from arrested development. But here — look, look at this rumpus of colour. Astonishing. Colour without prettiness, form without a single easy placement or easy line. Everything, you say, is new and strange. Look harder, I say, and you will find that it becomes old and familiar. You will find nature's primeval elements laid bare.'

She could only have been speaking of Charlie's work. Frank Siers's was not like that at all. I would not have been surprised to learn he'd meant to show up Charlie and prove that her teacher still knew best, but she threw him neck and crop. Put him in the shade with her colour, side-lined him with her composition. Perhaps he had an edge in draughtsmanship; he had more tact. Yet at his own show, in his studio, she pushed him into second place.

I write as if I liked her paintings on display (the one of James and Violet was not there). I tried to see them with a friendly eye, yet I found them ugly and ill bred. There was, Mrs Lendrum told us, a Cubist influence. I could see it — a ramshackle pedalling after

Cézanne and Picasso. Fragmented shapes, pieces of things tipped sideways, defying gravity. I am being unfair. I've heard and read explanations of this style — but it's all bizarrerie and nothing is put in to please. Nothing's beautiful.

Charlie showed her nude studies as well. As these things go, they were not excessively bare. Some were done on paper, in what I believe is called oil wash, and those, especially, exhibited a flowing line, not unpleasing. But wasn't there an ignorance of anatomy? Eric stood by my side and tutored me: 'See them as paintings, not as people.' That's all very well, easy to say, but the eye must proceed through habit and familiarity to an understanding of the new or we're at sea. There's nothing to wrap the mind around. One steps in the hole, incomprehension. A face, four limbs, a torso: don't you need those parts to make a person?

I did not like naked men and women bathing together, even though their backs were turned.

'Bolshevism,' said old Harold Fine behind us. He would be writing the review for the *Dominion*.

Frank Siers sold half a dozen. Charlie sold two, at five pounds each.

'Who would buy a thing like that?' I whispered to Rose.

'Me,' she said. 'And before you go off half-cocked, I used my nest egg, Sam. My own money.'

'What nest egg? Don't I provide? Rose, that thing —'

'— is a woman standing in a pool. Calm down. I like the way she's so still. And the water's still. I think I want to look at it for a long time. Sam,' she whispered, 'it made the hairs on my neck stand up.'

'Is there any need . . . any need . . . ?' I meant for this sort of thing, in a world where knowledge was plain and beauty never more than a head's turn away, and truth somehow — wasn't it proven? — the product of those two and the sum of art; and what could a half-woman in a muddy pond contribute to this hallowed stepping forth?

108

'Don't gabble, Sam. Don't talk nonsense. I don't like those ones that are broken in bits. I don't see the point. But I do see the point of this — at least I think I do. And I bought it with my money.'

'It's your sister, isn't it? That damned May.'

Rose went red. Suddenly she was angrier than I'd ever seen her. 'Do you think I can't do anything by myself? I'm going home. No, I'll walk. I don't need you.'

Out she went, a stranger to me; and, of course, I followed, desperate to bring us together again, which I accomplished, with the rain's help, although each of us is a different person now . . . It isn't in my story, so I'll leave it.

In my dashing out I collided on the stairs with James. Eric told me that he circled the room. People made way for him. The party chatter fell away. His shoes made a mensural ticking on the floor. Charlie watched, pale in her forehead, red in her cheeks; she advanced a half-step at him, half-raised her hands, but he went by, eyes turned to her paintings, which people stepped aside from so he could see; and when he'd made his round of the room and reached the door he found Frank Siers with his eyes, gave a nod of thanks — gentleman James — and went out from the fog of silence he had made.

Out into the first lashing of rain, where Lennie Ferrabee waited in the car. They drove away.

It was the night of the southerly storm — the great downpour, the drenching and thrashing of the city by wind and rain. Water soaked Rose and me to the skin, it ran inside our clothes, as we made our way home — I ten steps behind at first, then at her side, then holding her, holding on to lamp-posts and railings to stay upright. It came like a fist-blow from the south and knocked down trees. It turned streams into rivers, humping and leaping, and brought down cuttings across roads. Going up Hobson Street, we were lifted and propelled, and tried to stay like beetles close to the pavement in some layer of stillness that might survive down there, but felt the storm poised like a boot over us, and held each other and ran for our gate, our path, our door.

In night clothes and slippers and dressing-gowns we sat by the fire, I drinking whisky and she port, when there came a banging on our door, and Charlie and May and Eric tumbled in. They had come from the studio in Eric's car to find where we had vanished to, and on the way had learned that trees were down in Wadestown and the suburb was cut off.

'We'll have to stay here,' May said.

'Yes, yes,' Rose cried.

But Eric borrowed my oilskin — failed to get my gumboots on — and went out into the storm to see if his house was standing upright. It was the sort of adventure he loved.

'I wonder if Da got home,' Charlie said.

'Shall I telephone?'

'No, best not. He hates it when people fuss.'

I rang all the same but the operator told me a line was down on the Hutt Road.

Eric came back. The house was all right. The footbridge was plunging like a whaling boat, he said. 'Come and see.'

I refused. He stood dripping water, Captain Ahab, in my hall, and I stripped him of his oilskin, talked him out of his shoes, told him I had whisky and hot water in the next room, led him in with trousers rolled up and white cold feet, sat him down close to the fire. He was set to tell the women how brave he had been but they did not want to hear, for Charlie was weeping about her father — his cold cruel circling of Frank Siers's studio, and more, and more, all his coldnesses and cruelties, and why, why should she go on wanting his approval, wanting love?

'All the time I was away I was tied to him. Every time I lift my brush he's standing in the way . . .' A herd of complaints, contradictory, complementary, on and on; and Ferrabee too, battened on James, leeched on to him, helping with his overcoat and scarf, fetching his umbrella, opening this door and the next, carrying tea to his study on a tray, and saying with his sly grin, 'Yes, Sir James' — 'Sir' his joke — 'hunky-dory, sir.' He was butler, valet, chauffeur, handyman, sycophant. 'I hate him,' Charlie said. He drove James to his office and came back; lay smoking on his bed in a corner of the garage, only a wall's thickness from her as she worked; or he was in the kitchen, frying eggs, in the bathroom shaving, and once his face appeared in her window as she was dressing. 'Saw nothing, Miss Tinling, cross my heart,' he cried. He pranced on up the ladder to clean dead leaves from the gutters on the roof.

'Does James allow this?' May said.

'I haven't told him. Anyway, he never hears. He doesn't hear me.'

'What about Vi? What does she say?'

'She's frightened of him. Ferrabee's got a way of not being there, and suddenly there. She says to me, "Who is he? What does he want?" She told Da once there was a strange man in the house, but he just said, "He works for me." So Mother stays in her room. As long as I'm there, or Mrs Hearn or Mrs Dyer . . .'

'She's there tonight?'

'Yes. Mother quite likes her. She's more refined than Mrs Hearn.' Charlie, after all her tears, managed to smile.

'I'll telephone again in the morning,' I told her. 'If there's no reply we'll go out.'

The house shuddered and the ceiling groaned. Rose said we should all try to get some rest. She had beds prepared and night clothes warming. So we slept, all of us fitfully, as the storm raked the house and bent the window glass.

The weather was subdued in the morning: a supportable wind, unmalicious rain. When I looked in the street, the gutters were running quarter full. I tried telephoning James's house but lines were still down.

'We'll all go,' May said. 'See the damage.'

Eric had to dry the sparking plugs first. We set out shortly after nine o'clock. I see it as a crossing — but I won't get ahead, or send my sensibilities nosing into the past, where they'll only put things out of shape. Let me stay with journalism. Spray from the sea splashed over us. We went chassis deep through flooded streets — so on, so on. James's gate was open. His driveway was mushy with silt. Eric crept the car underneath the portico. The house seemed empty. May, finding the front door unlocked, strode in; and down in the kitchen we found the man Ferrabee frying eggs, as Charlie had described.

'Didn't hear you knock,' he said aggressively.

'Where's Da?' Charlie demanded. 'Where's Mrs Dyer?'

'He's in his study. She went home last night. She was worried about her nippers in the storm. I had to drive her.'

'What about Mother? Where's she?'

'Haven't seen her this morning. Mind if I eat my eggs?'

Charlie ran up the stairs. Eric and I knocked on James's study door. He half rose when he saw us. 'Eric. Sam. Has something gone wrong?'

We explained that we had come to see if he had reached home safely, but got no further, for Charlie came clattering down. 'She's not in her room. Mother, where are you?' she called.

'What?' said James, confused to find his house full of women.

'Where's she gone?'

'Not upstairs? Have you tried the bathroom?'

'She's not there. She's slept in her bed but it's cold. Where is she, Da?'

'I've no idea. Would she go outside? Ferrabee. See if Mrs Tinling is in the grounds. Have you looked everywhere, Girl? Tried all the rooms? You don't think she'd get into a cupboard somewhere?'

112

We searched the house, then Eric and I paddled down the garden paths and squelched across the lawns. We looked in the garage, where Ferrabee had made a bivouac in a corner; tried Charlie's studio door but found it locked. Ferrabee was nosing in the ngaio trees.

'Vanishimo,' he said.

We walked along the side of the stream, which ran fast and muscly between its entry hole in one brick wall and its exit in the other. It had fallen from its night-time high, marked by a line of leaves and twigs on the lawn.

'She's not here,' we told them in the house.

James repeated what he had told the women: he had sent Mrs Dyer home with Ferrabee, had looked in and seen Violet sleeping, had sent Ferrabee to bed when he came back, and then sat up turning things over and listening to the storm for half the night. Turning what over? Was it Charlie's paintings or his whole life? He seemed to me brought to a point or edge. There was a strange colour in his face, and something almost bloodied in his manner — a pulse of life undisciplined? He said, 'She never rang her bell. But of course I wouldn't hear it in the storm.'

'You said she came down though,' May said.

'Yes, she did. About two o'clock. I saw her there, in the door, so I asked her what the matter was, and she said there was too much noise and the house kept moving. She said it was turning round to face the other way. I told her it was only the storm and not to worry. She asked for Mrs Dyer and I told her she'd gone home, she was worried about her children being alone. Violet didn't seem to know she even had any children. I helped her back upstairs, into bed. I tucked her in.' James looked surprised. 'I got her another pillow and told her to go to sleep. She said she would. Then I went to bed. And that's all. I can't understand how she got downstairs again.'

'Were any doors open?' Eric said.

113

'I lock everything when I'm finished for the night. But the back one was. I thought it was Ferrabee. He comes and goes.'

'Shouldn't we be searching?' Charlie cried. 'Or shouldn't we get the police?'

'Oh, no police,' James said. 'She'll just have wandered away.' He frowned himself back to his usual state. 'I don't want this getting out. Sam?' He meant could I keep it out of the newspapers.

'We'd better start asking at the neighbours',' Eric said.

Then Ferrabee came shouting over the lawn: 'Mr Tinling.' He skidded through the doorway, almost falling on his knees. 'She's in the creek.'

We ran through the garden, through the trees, to the hole in the wall where the stream ran out. Iron bars, six inches apart, stopped large debris from getting through. Torn branches lay tangled against them like pick-up-sticks. A whirlpool sucked the water down in front. Eric and I had seen nothing there, but now we saw, all of us, Violet's arm like a branch stripped of its bark. It nestled among others, curved and white. Her hair was wrapped about a torn fence paling that turned and slid in the current, showing half her face, then hiding it.

Ferrabee climbed like a monkey on the bars. I held a ngaio branch, gripped Eric's hand, and he waded in. Between them, they freed Violet and dragged her, white and girlish, on to the lawn. She was naked, colder than the water that had held her down. Eric took his jacket from where he had thrown it on the lawn and covered her. He picked her up like a sleeping child and carried her to the house, up the stairs, laid her on the bed; then we, Eric and I, withdrew. Left her there with James and Charlie and May and Rose. We joined Ferrabee in the kitchen, and soon James came down the stairs and went into his study and closed the door.

'Doctor and police?' Eric said after a while.

'What's the hurry? Can't bring her back,' Ferrabee said.

He took a tray of tea to the study, then went out to the garage to change his clothes.

'You'd better get something dry on, Eric,' I said.

'I've been wet so often lately I don't see the point.' He found another pot and made tea, swallowed it. 'Do you think she walked in or fell?'

'Fell,' I said.

'Not Ferrabee?'

'No. Good God, no. Why would he?'

'All right,' he said.

I've looked at it so many ways — that James had seen her go and turned his back; that terror overcame her in the house that moved, where her life had turned her from the happy girl, triumphant bride, into the faded woman, querulous and afraid, of her last days, turned her about, and so she had fled into the storm and found the boiling stream and killed herself — but I prefer to think now that she simply had no will to stay alive. She left the house where her life had already ended and was lashed by wind and rain outside the door; walked barefooted in strange elements; came to the stream and did not understand; perhaps even tried to walk across, it was so different from anything she had known. When the water got too strong she let it rush her down, and when she reached the iron grille and found herself trapped there, had no thought of living or dying but only of waiting for what came next — if she had any thought at all.

It's something more than a game I play; I'm half convinced.

Another possibility: when James tucked her in, his tenderness unhinged her.

Eric said, 'We'd better see James.'

He was lighting a fire in the study and frowned when we came in.

'We're going to have to let someone know,' Eric said.

'I've tried the phone. It's still dead. Perhaps you could ask Ferrabee to fetch the doctor?'

'He'll have to bring the police as well. James, we want to say how sorry —'

'She had a disappointing life,' he said. 'I tried my best but there was no making her happy. Heaven knows —' he looked at us suddenly, penetrating — 'I racked my brains. You all saw that. She was no help in my career. Nevertheless . . .'

He seemed on the point of expressing pity but turned to the fire instead and puffed air from the bellows on to the kindling sticks.

'How are the women taking it?'

'We'll go and see. James you can come and stay with us for a while.'

'Whatever for? Charlotte will be here. That's all I need. There'll be lots of fuss, I suppose. Is there no way of keeping the police out?'

'James . . .'

'Yes, I see. It's a death, after all. In unusual circumstances. Perhaps Ferrabee could go for them.'

I found him in the kitchen. Eric shifted his car to let him out, and he drove away. We went upstairs and tapped on Violet's door. Rose came out.

'We thought we should try something, but she was so cold,' she said.

'I think she'd been in there for hours,' Eric said. 'How —' He was going to ask about Charlie but said instead, 'How are you all?'

'I don't know. How are we? She's my sister, Eric.'

I held her as she cried . . . and I won't go on with this; with doctor and police and the women. With Violet's funeral, which was private. All of it is private, how we passed those days.

Charlie said, 'I can't leave Da alone.' She went back home with him. James had not invited us for any sort of gathering or wake — for anything post-Violet. We went to our own homes and closed the doors behind us.

When the stream went down Ferrabee found Violet's nightie tangled in the broken branches at the grille.

Eight

Forbes and Coates were back from London where they had attended the King's Silver Jubilee. Forbes had not announced an election date, although the Coalition's four-year term was up in December. He had grabbed an extra year in 1934, using the collapsed economy as an excuse, but would not be able to do it a second time.

Eric and I ran into Oliver Joll at a rugby match and put the question to him: when would it be?

'Gentlemen, if I knew...' He spread his hands, then laughed and apologised. 'I'm not pretending, Sam. I'm learning about life as the new boy. Nobody tells me.'

'I warned you.'

'Patience is the thing. I don't mind as long as I can help beat these blighters.' He meant Labour. 'Well, I'm off. It's a pretty poor game. Oh, butterfingers, keep your eye on the ball. He's a ninny, that boy. Goodbye, Sam. Goodbye, Professor.' Off he went in his cashmere overcoat and brown Homburg hat — a bit of a dandy, Oliver Joll. Then he was back. 'I was so sorry, it knocked me sideways — Mrs Tinling. A terrible thing. I wrote James a letter. Terrible thing. And of course, she was your sister-in-law. My sympathies.' It seemed straight shooting, not politics. He strode away.

The player he had called a ninny was our nephew, Taylor Barr.

He played on the wing for College Old Boys and scored a try shortly after Ollie Joll left — not a good try, all he had to do was fall on the ball. I spotted Owen Moody in a seat further down the stand, pointed him out to Eric and we went down.

'Muddied oafs,' Owen said. 'Can you see the attraction? You'd think the ball had a personality. They're loving it one minute and kicking it the next.'

I asked him why he hadn't been in touch. I needed to talk about our novel and sort out where it was going and how to bring it there.

'Who's left in?'

'You and me. Theo Mead. Four or five others. Euan Poynter is out.'

'So am I,' Eric said. 'You can keep my bit about the poison, that's all. I think your man with the scar would be a poisoner.'

I saw a blue intemperance, flash of anger, in Owen's eyes. 'I don't know about that.'

'We can't talk about it here. Can you come and see me, Owen?'

'Yes, well. Not next week. Maybe after that. I'll drop you a note.'

'Oh, that hurt,' Eric said. Taylor lay writhing on the ground.

'He'll get no sympathy from me,' Owen said.

'He's putting it on,' I said.

'Of course he is. There's the whistle. Now he has to wash off all his mud. Thank God for cricket.'

Eric dropped me at my gate, where I met Frank Siers coming out.

'I've been delivering Mrs Holloway's painting,' he said. 'And asking about poor Charlotte. What a sad thing. Is she all right? Mrs Holloway didn't seem at all sure.'

Her mother's dead, of course she's not all right, I wanted to say. 'Ninny' seemed a fitter word for Siers than for Taylor Barr. He quivered away.

Rose had hung the painting in the room where she did her sewing. 'It's out of your way here,' she said.

She had overlooked — or perhaps she hadn't — that I was in and out all the time and would see it baring its moony flesh at me ten times a day.

'I asked Charlotte to come across and see it. She's going to ride her bicycle in tomorrow.'

'All that way?'

'She's a big strong girl. It's not her I'm worried about. I know she feels she should have helped Vi more. Stayed at home instead of traipsing around doing sketches. Mr Siers rang her and all she could do was cry. I think it's just a scouring out. She'll be all right. But James . . .' His coldness, self-absorption, were a mortal disease. 'They were married forty years and it's as if he's said goodbye to some visitor at the gate.'

Rose looked at Charlie's painting and I wondered what that naked figure would come to mean. If you turned her round, would she wear Vi's face?

The rain began again next morning, spoiling Charlie's plan to cycle in from the Hutt. She walked to Melling station and caught a train. At half past ten she stood cold and dripping at our door. Rose dried her and gave her clothes. They talked in the sewing room for an hour — too long to spend admiring a painting. It was Charlie's dilemma detaining them: she could not leave her father, but must if she was to have a life of her own.

Duty holds one in a vise. But how the argument widens out. Any worthwhile dictionary identifies half a dozen kinds. What did Charlie owe James? Obedience and submission, he would have said. He would have her 'duteous'. She, I'm sure, when all the pain of neglect was taken away, still wanted — needed — to love him.

Charlie stays; she cannot go until there occurs some further act, whether of love or something else, that she must make and he accept, or he must make to dismiss and free her: so I concluded on that morning in my study, while she and Rose talked in the sewing room — then chattered in there, laughed in there.

I gave away my analysis — had meant to see if I might somehow raise the matter at lunch. Instead I talked crossly about modern art, saying that Stanley Spencer mutilated the human form, creating no more than a human burlesque, and the Royal Academy had been perfectly right to reject his paintings; which Charlie bridled at and we had a set-to. Rose finished it by telling me to take my sore head away from the table. I sat in my study and grew contrite: what a time to bully the girl, with her mother scarcely two weeks dead.

The rain eased to a drizzle. We took umbrellas and walked up the hill to visit May and Eric. He and I grew careless of our differences and fell into a quarrel about poetry, I quoting with distaste: 'the sparrows in the gutters' — 'You cannot,' I cried, 'you cannot use gutters in poetry' — and 'smell of steak in passageways' and 'yellow soles of feet'.

'He's got some malady,' I said, 'some pathological twisting in his bowels. It's little,' I said, 'it's unlovely, and worst of all it's unmusical. Don't they have ears, don't they have eyes? And isn't there one, just one, happy man amongst them? Now listen. Listen to this:

' "Read from some humble poet,
Whose songs gushed from his heart —" '
Eric interrupted:
' "And the cares that infest the day
Shall fold their tents, like the Arabs,
And as silently steal away."
'That's very nice, but isn't it yesterday's language, Sam?'
'It's not, it's eternal.' I wouldn't be stopped. Recited:
' "When all the world is young, lad,
And all the trees are green . . ." (Charles Kingsley) and:

' "Jenny kissed me when we met,

Jumping from the chair she sat in . . ." ' (Leigh Hunt).

'There's a sensualist inside you, Sam, elbowing to get out.' He almost never resorted to sneering. (The women, like Arabs, had silently stolen away.)

Suddenly calm, I said, 'That's unworthy, Eric. That's not like you.'

'No, I'm sorry. Care for a walk? I need some air.'

We climbed the hill, sharing an umbrella.

'I've done something stupid. I'm in trouble,' he said. 'I would have mentioned it yesterday but I needed to talk to May.'

I felt, simultaneously, elation and dread. Eric had confided in me but never confessed before.

'I went to visit Lily Maxey on Friday night. Just for a yack, that's all we do. We were talking about that Clara Butt concert and she asked me if I'd like to go next door. They were having a musical evening — it's true, Sam, they were. Lily plays the piano really well and one of the girls takes singing lessons in the day. She's got a voice a bit like Jenny Lind, very pure. So I went. It was foolish, I know. But I've told May. She understands.'

'What happened?'

'It's not really a brothel, not like one. Although the girls weren't wearing very much. But Lily played the piano and Susan, that's the singing girl, she sang. We played some records and one or two people danced. Then I sang — you know how I like to when I get the chance. "Drink to me only", I sang that. A bad choice, really. It's better for a tenor than a baritone. But in the middle of it the police raided the place.'

The rain had stopped. I made a business of shaking and folding my umbrella. I doubted Eric. I doubted he was telling the whole truth. Gutters, I thought, yellow soles. We seemed, on top of our hill, like two wrinkled dwarves in baggy clothes.

123

'It's lucky you were singing,' I said.

'I meant to leave sooner. I was leaving. But you know how I am — one last song, when people ask.'

'Did they arrest you?'

'No, they don't do that, not with the men. They took our names. There were officers from a liner in port. And one or two others.'

'Who?'

'I can't tell you names. No one you're friends with.'

'Except you. Who did they arrest?'

'Lily and three of the girls. One of them had her husband there. They let her go.'

'It is a brothel though, isn't it? That's what it's for?'

'Yes, but it wasn't in use. I swear that, Sam. It might have been later — it would have been. But no one used the bedrooms when I was there. The police looked in — no one there. They weren't too pleased. There were five of them, a sergeant and four constables. They must have heard me singing. If they'd waited till I'd gone . . . I was all set to leave.'

'Was Mrs Maxey leaving?'

'Yes, she would have, back next door. She doesn't go in when they don't need her.'

'That's why they raided, then. They wanted to get the owner. The girls are prostitutes, aren't they?'

Eric sighed. He turned away. 'Yes, they are.' We stood in silence, yellow dwarves. 'But they're pleasant girls. Nothing common. One of them used to be a teacher. Kindergarten, she says. And one of them sings.'

'As well as that they have sex for money. And Mrs Maxey gets her share. I suppose she's rich?'

'Not as much as some of the crooked businessmen in town, friends of yours. So don't get moral. I was there to visit Lily, and later on for the music and maybe a dance. I think I danced. Yes, once. I like it, all right? But I didn't do a single thing ... You don't believe me.'

'Yes, I do.' I believed him. 'Does May?'

He nodded. 'She's furious. Did you see?'

'I thought she was just out of sorts.'

'At least she knows I didn't misbehave. I told you, Sam, May and I ... The trouble is, I just do damn fool things.'

'I imagine she's jealous of Mrs Maxey.'

'No, she's not.'

'I mean because you talk to her.'

'I talk to May. You've heard how we talk. How we trust each other.'

It was not enough. He must flirt with carnality and abasement. He must go close and open his nostrils to the smell. It was part of his largeness, he might say; and I would say it wasted and reduced him.

'So,' I said, after a while, 'what happens now?'

'They'll be in court tomorrow. Magistrates Court.'

'Charged with what?'

'Keeping a house of ill fame, I suppose. That's Lily. The others — I don't know. Working there. I don't know what they call it. She's got a lawyer. He says she'll get bail, so that's all right. The thing is, he wants to call some of the men.'

'Mightn't the prosecution want them too?'

'Wybrow, he's her lawyer, doesn't think so. A couple of them are stuffed-shirt boys.' He gave an angry laugh. 'They've got their businesses to attend to.'

'So if Wybrow calls you ... ?'

Eric looked at me over his glasses. 'I've known Lily for a long time, Sam.'

I nodded. He would stand up in court and testify that his brothel-keeping friend had played the piano and he had sung Ben Jonson's song. That was where his stupidity led. If they asked him what the house was used for when the singing stopped, what would he say?

'It's touch and go. Wybrow thinks the police might have to drop their charges.'

'Meanwhile you get tarred with a dirty brush.'

'That doesn't matter. It doesn't matter. May knows what I am. You know what I am.' He peered at me and I turned away. I did not know. He had been firm under my feet, then less firm as our sad and ugly year went on, and now honest affections were all he had left. They gave him little weight.

I'm mixing my metaphors. Journalists should avoid them — although I'm more than a journalist now. It seems I'm that novelist I wanted to make a twelfth part of. Novelists can use metaphors, and beat them together like butter and eggs if they choose.

Where was I? Nowhere, that's the truth. The rain started again. I put up my umbrella and shared it with Eric, although I did not want his shoulder rubbing mine. Back at the house, he offered to drive Charlie home. Rose and I walked down the hill to Hobson Street. May had not told her of Eric's evening out. I did not tell her either: the time would come.

I apologised for my nasty temper that day.

I did not go to court, and would have wasted my time if I had, for the magistrate cleared it because of 'the very many unsavoury details in the case'. He allowed representatives of the Society for the Protection of Women and Children to stay.

I'll have done with it, although it dragged on for two days. Eric was not called to testify. The magistrate dismissed the charges for lack of evidence. A triumph for the lawyers and a defeat for the rule of law. The only good thing to come out of it was that Mrs

Maxey closed the 'house' part of her house. She put the whole property on the market.

Enough of her. She'll come back when it's time.

The public felt cheated, or so my friends in the newspaper business claimed. It's closer to the truth to say they felt cheated. Only *Truth* followed up the story — hints and insinuations and moral outrage, with the hypocrisy that makes me ashamed of my calling sometimes. It wasn't for long. Another, and greater, sensation soon turned up.

Why am I being cryptic? It's writing cheques when you've got no money in the bank. That's what I learn as I sit scribbling here.

Out in the open then, laying it down flat: on Friday of that week I called in to pass the time with friends in the reporters' room at the *Dominion*. Alan Gooch, who did arts and entertainments, called me over.

'We decided not to run Harold Fine's review of your niece's art show. In view of her mother, you know. It was pretty savage.'

I thanked him. 'How did Harold take it?'

'Not well.'

The telephone rang in the chief reporter's cubicle — Dinny Thompson. Strange in those places when a story breaks: a tremor runs through, a silence falls and only a single voice is heard. Dinny, still holding the phone, put out his head and yelled, 'Clarry, George, pronto. Get over to Ollie Joll's office. Someone's been shot.'

I did not run with them. My days are over for that. When Dinny came out, I said, 'Who?'

'He doesn't know. Not Ollie. He's all right. It looks like he's the one who did the shooting though. My man's not sure.'

James, I thought. 'Is someone dead?'

'Looks like it. 'Scuse me, Sam.'

I went down to the street and walked past the library and the town hall. The police had cleared the bottom of Taranaki Street. Broken glass and a broken chair lay on the footpath by Joll's door. Men eased out with a stretcher and fed it into an ambulance. I could not see the person's face but knew enough about how ambulance men behave to realise that he — she? — was still alive.

Ollie Joll came out with two policemen. He wore his cashmere coat and Homburg hat — immaculate. His face was — how was it? I could not get close — ruined, and shifted to one side, dislocating him from the Ollie I had known.

The policemen put him in a car and drove away.

I saw Clarry Foley running for the *Dominion* and could not stop him. George Stone moved in the crowd, hunting witnesses.

'Who was it, George?'

'They won't say. But I heard one of the girls in the office. It's some young bloke — can't publish it — called Owen Moody.'

Nine

He did not die. The bullet, from a German pistol First Lieutenant Joll had brought home from the war, struck him high on the right side of his chest, nicked his lung and came to rest under his shoulder blade. The surgeon had only to make a cut in Owen's skin for it to pop out.

The charge against Oliver Joll, made before JPs the following day, was attempted murder. He was remanded until Monday, then remanded again in the Magistrates Court. It was two weeks before he was able to plead.

Taranaki Street. The crowd stood gawking, and I gawked along with them. I wanted to know and not know. I thought, It can't have happened, yet it had. Was Owen Moody a robber? Had Ollie Joll fired his shot in self-defence? That was the simplest explanation. I rejected it. 'Owen' and 'robber' failed to conjoin. He had the boldness for that role but wasn't stupid enough. Jealousy then? They had fought over a woman. I could see Joll and Owen in dispute — but over some bit of property, not for love. They were, it came to me, impure. The thing began in adulteration of some sort — with the creature each had made of himself. This shooting was the final act in a history. Neither was an accidental man.

131

How had they met...? So I went on, confusing, tormenting myself. I was stitched into their pattern and should be able to see the story of it all.

But things hidden there might injure me. Fear made me hesitate a moment. Then I hurried round to the D.I.C, where Taylor Barr worked in the menswear department. Someone quicker had beaten me with the news. Taylor had mounted his motorcycle and sped away.

'A friend has been in an accident, evidently. Mr Barr has gone to the hospital,' the head salesman told me.

I caught the Newtown tram. But why go on — I did this, I did that, it's not about me. Yet I've turned myself into a peg to hang it on. Well then: could not find Taylor at the hospital. Detectives had latched on to him and taken him away to hear his story, which contained neither much nor little: he shared a flat with Owen Moody, they were friends, he knew Mr Joll well enough to say hello, Owen had met him two or three weeks before... He repeated it to Eric and me when we drove around to Oriental Bay to see him that night.

Taylor had recovered from his shock. He was up in the air, buoyant with the drama and Owen's escape. The bullet had gone right through him and popped out like an orange pip when the doctor gave a squeeze. A week or two and he would be on his feet and raising Cain. Taylor mimed thanks to heaven, lifting his eyes. 'The merest half inch,' he told us, measuring.

'What we want to know, Taylor, is how Owen and Ollie Joll knew each other.'

'I introduced them. Mr Joll comes in and buys his shirts from me. Golly, we've lost a customer.'

'Introduced them in the shop?'

'Oh, no. Oh, no. At the football. We were playing at the Hutt

132

Recreation Ground. You often see Mr Joll at games, and Hutt is sort of next door to his electorate. It could be for votes, I never thought of that. Anyway, Owen was there watching me play. He doesn't like football, he's always saying that muddied oafs thing.'

'Another bit is flannelled fools,' Eric said.

'Yes. Owen says all the fools are on the other side. We were talking and Mr Joll came up and wished me luck, so I introduced them. I didn't think Owen would like him much, but they got on like a house on fire. We went and had dinner with him at the St George Hotel.'

'When?'

'One night that week. And Owen had dinner with him again, later on. He told me he'd asked him for a job and Mr Joll said he'd think about it.'

'What sort of job?'

'Well, Owen had worked it out that Mr Joll needs someone to run his business when he goes into Parliament. So he told Mr Joll he'd like to do it.'

'That's absurd. Owen can't run a business, he's a clerk.'

Taylor was offended. 'Owen's smart. He's smarter than all three of us put together, I'd say.'

'Is that what they quarrelled about? A job?'

'I don't know. I don't know what went on. All I know is Owen had an appointment to go and see him. He told me he had a good chance. It would be good pay.'

'And Ollie shot him?'

'High up. Here.' Taylor embedded his finger in his chest. 'He'll have a scar. Two scars. Front and back.'

'Ollie must have turned him down and Owen got upset.'

It was more believable than robbery.

Driving home, Eric said, 'You know who's going to take Joll's place in the Melling electorate?'

'James's lucky day,' I said.

'Good luck or bad?'

James did not want to talk about it. The whole thing had a bad smell. I could not very well reply that his party had no one else to turn to; said instead that people would understand if under the circumstances . . . I could not go on. But he chose to be offended by what I had said rather than what I had not.

'Circumstances?'

'I just mean —'

'There are no circumstances involving me. I stand completely aside from this — event. It's another country. The man is gone. He doesn't exist.'

'I see that —'

'And I won't have it said that I'm taking someone's place.'

'You remember Moody, though, the man who was shot?'

'The fellow on the motorcycle. You can tell Taylor to sever that connection.'

'James, your rule doesn't extend that far.'

'I'm busy, Sam. Please don't telephone me again.' He hung up.

After that, quietness from him, stillness out in the Hutt. But chatter, chatter everywhere else. The questions, speculations, mistaken 'facts', bits of false knowledge I heard in the two weeks before the true story came out — if I'd shovelled them up they would have filled the tray of a lorry. Some were as dull as puddles: Joll had caught Owen Moody hunting for cash in his desk drawer. Others cut like bits of broken glass: Owen was having an affair with Ollie's wife. Variations on the theme of money and sex. A kind of Joll-o-mania, Moody-mania, seized the town. Two of the questions asked were: Who is this Owen Moody? Where's he from? I learned that he was an American, that he was an unsuccessful actor, that he played the clarinet in a dance band, that he sponged off women, was a gigolo, that he was the son of an English earl — seriously, all of that, and more: that he raced motorbikes on the Isle of Man, that he 'fixed' racehorses for crooks. Bits of truth came out — he was a clerk at Barnhill Importers, a better-than-average cricketer, a would-be poet. I kept silent. I did not want it known that he was part of a group of men engaged in writing a detective story. Got hold of my fellow scribblers, told them to keep mum.

I sat at my desk reading our chapters: poor Roy's with its pomposities, so unlike him; Eric's full of neat dead sentences (unlike him), and its untraceable poison that left the victim smiling; Euan's cut and dried, balanced and clear, but shying away from the blood that should have flowed and the screams that should have rent the air; my own, ditto, shying away; Tom Gow's, fourth form stuff; Fred Scanlon's, butterfat and wool; and last, chapter eight, Owen Moody's.

It did not seem so very good now. Yet it stayed alive through the physical conviction driving it and the black counterflow of fear. I read it closely. I tried to lift stones. Who was this man with the scar that shone like a silver smile? Owen had met him in his dreams — and then drawn back from admitting more. But don't we all 'know' that our dreams reveal truths about ourselves that the daytime mind suppresses? Is that the latest word? Do I have it right? Well then, this scarred man with his unearthly beauty and the hatred that makes him kill, was he Owen's alter ego, the Mr Hyde to his cricket-playing Dr Jekyll? Had he emerged in Ollie Joll's office and forced poor Ollie to shoot?

I worked and worried at it but the stone would not shift. I circled around the way hyenas circle prey, but instead of closing in was pushed by lack of courage further away, and was able at last to resume my role as editor, give a mental tick to this bit of his chapter, purse my lips at that, and decide that Owen was really not so clever after all, for wouldn't the cigarette butt Rufus had picked up turn soggy on his swim to the motorboat and become useless as evidence?

I smiled with relief. Owen was taped. I bundled him up with the others, made him fast with a bulldog clip, and locked him in the bottom drawer of my study desk.

Eric was lecturing in Christchurch and could not come to the court. I would have preferred to remain alone but people I knew were all about. I sat down at last with two of my defaulters, Euan Poynter and Tom Gow — no getting away. Dudley Aimer was several rows in front, already drawing furtively on a pad — which Freddie Barr, two along, peered to see. Taylor stayed outside with the witnesses, although he was unlikely to be called.

The magistrate was J. W. Mander, a man who likes no sound but soft breathing in his court. He looks up frowning if a seat creaks or a pencil drops. A shout of agreement or disbelief makes him clear the room; yet I saw him send his handkerchief once — so clean and white, it sparkled — to a woman sobbing in the witness stand.

He had to put up with creaking seats, exhaled breath, indrawn breath when the court guards brought Ollie Joll to the prisoner's box. Ollie stood straight. We needed confrontation, and peered around, dabbing our heads this way and that, for Owen Moody. Without Ollie's victim — his antagonist? his partner? — there was a great lacuna in proceedings. It was like a wedding without the bride, a wrestling match where one of the contestants fails to show up.

Ollie was dressed in his usual natty way, but did not seem to fit his skin. 'Seem', I say, because our perception was at fault. He was steady, he was square. He kept still. He meant to give no satisfaction. Yet we shrank him, darkened him; we blurred his image with the suppositions we held and the half-truths we knew.

'Where's Moody?' Euan Poynter whispered.

'I remember him from school. He was pretty iffy even then,' Tom Gow said.

'Is he still in hospital?'

'No, he's home,' I said, knowing it from Taylor, who had taken time off work to look after him. (Owen's mother, Taylor informed me with a grin, had come steaming up from Christchurch 'like the royal yacht', but Owen had got rid of her 'toot sweet'.)

'He's well enough to be here, I'll bet,' Tom Gow said. 'He was always doing a bunk from things at school.'

'Shhh,' Euan said. The magistrate was frowning.

I frown. I wrinkle my brows at the problem I face: how to put it down. I've got clippings from the *Dominion* and the *Evening Post* and *Truth* to help me if my memory fails, and I've got my (unfailing) memories of that day. The path I need to follow lies between them or I'll end up on scaly ground or sinking in a bog. Where's the path? I see it running on, but where does it begin; and when it has led me as far as it goes, isn't there a second path that carries on, a harder one, a crueller one, clinging to a cliff-face where I dare not look down?

I must put this stuff out of my mind.

Colin Brookes, a Harbour Board employee, was walking on the footpath opposite Joll's office in Taranaki Street when he heard a gunshot. The time was 1.55 in the afternoon. He stopped with several other passers-by, wondering if the sound might be a truck backfiring. A carrier, Mr Sidley, working in a loading bay, said no, he was a returned soldier and he knew a pistol shot when he heard it. They were trying to work out where the sound had come from when the glass shattered in Joll's window across the street and a chair came hurtling out and landed on the pavement. A young man appeared in the window. 'Help me, I've been shot,' he cried. As Brookes crossed the street, he saw two men struggling in the room. Five more gunshots sounded.

Michael O'Meara, a storeman, was talking with the typiste, Miss Bird, in Joll's ground-floor office when a shot sounded from upstairs. He ran to the door and saw Joll appear on the landing. 'Fetch an ambulance, O'Meara. Mr Moody has shot himself,' Joll cried. At that moment a crashing sound came, and pieces of broken glass fell on the pavement outside, followed by a chair. Joll ran back into his office. O'Meara heard cries and a struggle, then the sound of further gunshots. He told Miss Bird to call the police, then started up the stairs, hesitating.

Brookes and Sidley ran past O'Meara. It was like going over the top at Flers, Sidley said. Joll appeared on the landing and stood aside to let them pass. 'Be careful of him, he's badly hurt,' he said.

Moody was sitting on the floor, with his back resting against Joll's desk. He held a pistol in his lap and his head was slumped forward. The front of his shirt was covered in blood. As the men approached, he looked up and said, 'Mr Joll has shot me. Get a car and take me to a doctor.' Sidley took the pistol and laid it on Joll's desk. Moody appeared to faint. He lay on his side.

Joll said, 'I was showing him my pistol and it accidentally went off and he shot himself.'

The two men carried Moody downstairs, where he recovered

consciousness and said, 'I have discovered a scandal. Give my love to my mother.' He fainted again.

Miss Bird, who knew first aid from the Girl Guides, used the office scissors to cut open Moody's shirt. She examined the wound in his chest. Moody woke again and said he was dying. Miss Bird told him the injury was not that bad and that he should lie still and not talk.

Seeing the wounded man was in good hands, Brookes went upstairs to check if Joll was all right. He found him putting some papers into his safe. Joll said he was tidying up and asked if 'young Moody' was going to 'make it'. Brookes told him he had better come downstairs. Miss Bird had made Moody comfortable. Joll said, 'Guns are dangerous things. He didn't have any experience.'

They waited for the ambulance to arrive.

When Constable David McAndrew arrived at Joll's office he found Moody lying at the foot of the stairs, with Miss Bird supporting his head. The accused, Joll, was standing nearby. He had his hands in his pockets and appeared calm. Several other people were present, including the previous witnesses.

McAndrew asked Joll if the shooting was an accident. 'Of course it was. He was playing with my Mauser and it went off. Then he fell against the window and it broke.'

Sergeant Peter Burrell arrived with three more constables. They questioned witnesses while an ambulance took the wounded man away. Joll waited in the downstairs office.

Burrell examined the room upstairs, where he took possession of a pistol. He locked the door and drove Joll to the police station. On the way Joll said, 'Good God, Peter, what a mistake. He was an amateur. I should never have let him fiddle with that thing. I brought it back from the war, you know.' He also said, 'I believe that poor young man will die.'

Senior Sergeant Trevor Dowling questioned Joll at the station. Joll repeated that Moody had been playing with the pistol; he was spinning it on his finger 'like Tom Mix' when it went off. The shot threw him back against the window, which broke. When Joll was trying to help him, Moody pulled the trigger several more times, by some sort of automatic action of his finger.

Joll asked if there was any news from the hospital.

Dowling said, 'I have abundant evidence that a serious disturbance took place in your office. Before the shots were heard, a chair was thrown through the window on to the street.'

'What chair? Who says?'

'The carriers on the stand across the street.'

'My God,' Joll said.

Dowling charged him with attempted murder.

How long can I keep on in this way? It is like demonstrating that one and one makes two, when the real question is being not number. What is 'one', who is he, who is the other, and when they're brought together, what is the nature of 'two'?

In one of his talks, Eric described the 'whirling coalescence' that results when two stars approaching each other become so deeply involved that gravitation prevents their escape. Their velocity increases; their paths change from rectilinear to hyperbolic, with the focus of each orbit at the centre of the other star. Then comes the tidal distortion, the flinging out of mass that makes our planets, which take form about the new sun...

The court rose for lunch. I walked on the wharves, watching gulls float and dip and water slide about the piles. It had a thickened movement beneath its oily sheen. 'Whirling coalescence' played in my mind but brought no useful insight. Dudley Aimer joined me, eating a meat pie. He showed me sketches he had made of Ollie Joll — some realistic, some caricature. Handsome Oliver: I preferred those to big-toothed Ollie, gun-toting Ollie.

'He's not an easy man to draw. He's nothing when you do him straight, but you lose him when you pull bits out of shape,' Dudley said. 'He's impressive though, don't you think, just sitting there looking straight ahead.'

'Something terrible must have happened,' I said.

'It's women or money. We'll find out.'

Miss Jean Bird, typiste, had first seen the man she now knew to be Owen Moody three days before the shooting. He came to the office one afternoon with Mr Joll. The two appeared to be on friendly terms. They laughed and joked going up the stairs and stayed talking in the office for more than an hour. While there they drank some whisky, because Miss Bird found empty glasses smelling of liquor on Mr Joll's desk when she tidied up before going home. She took them downstairs to rinse.

She next saw Owen Moody on the Thursday of that week, shortly after lunch. He and Mr Joll came in at two o'clock. Mr Joll smelled of liquor but that was not unusual as he often took a glass of beer with his lunch, even when he ate a sandwich upstairs in his office. The two men were in good spirits and Mr Joll said, 'Watch this young fellow, Jean. He's got an eye for a pretty girl.'

Mr Joll closed the office door. At about three o'clock she took up some letters to be signed. When she knocked, Mr Joll opened

the door and said before she could speak, 'Later, Jean. Not now.'
He seemed agitated. His face was pale.

A short while later Miss Bird heard angry voices from upstairs,
then nothing more until about 4 p.m. when the two men came down.
Owen Moody was leading. He handed Miss Bird a sealed envelope
and asked her to take it to the Post Office and have it registered. Mr
Joll said, 'Yes, Jean. Please do it.' The men went upstairs again.

Miss Bird took the letter as instructed. It was addressed to Owen
Moody at Wellington Central Post Office.

Mr Moody left at about 4.30 p.m. He asked if she had the letter
receipt and when she handed it to him said, 'Good girl,' and
winked at her.

She took Mr Joll's letters up to him. He was standing with his
back to her, looking out the window. He told her to leave them on
his desk. He was still upstairs when she went home at 5 p.m.

The following day, the Friday of the shooting, Mr Joll behaved
in his normal manner. He was cheerful and busy. Owen Moody
arrived at 1.30. He went into Mr Joll's office without knocking and
closed the door. Miss Bird heard nothing for half an hour. Then
she heard a gunshot.

When Senior Sergeant Dowling charged him with attempted
murder, Joll said, 'Some mistake has been made.' He submitted to
being searched, then asked to call his lawyer.

Meanwhile Sergeant Burrell searched Joll's office. Broken glass
littered the floor beside the window overlooking Taranaki Street.
Joll's high-backed chair was lying on its side; an inkwell had spilled
ink on the desk which, judging from indentation marks in the
linoleum, had been shifted from its usual place, possibly during
the struggle described by previous witnesses. Five pistol shells lay

on the floor and one was located beneath a roll-top desk. They were later found to fit the accused's Mauser pistol. Three pellets went through the wall, another lodged in the spine of a book, and a fifth was found embedded in the angle of the skirting board and the floor.

Burrell searched Joll's desk, where he found business papers and two novels, one by Sapper and one by Zane Grey, borrowed from a threepenny library. He also found a framed photograph of Joll's wife and daughters in a bottom drawer, along with a pack of playing cards and several articles on political matters torn from newspapers. A small bottle of whisky and two glasses were found in the cupboard on the other side. The roll-top desk held writing materials.

Burrell opened the safe with the key sent round from the station after Joll had been searched. He found an envelope containing five photographs of naked women, three of naked men, and one of a man and woman engaged in lewd activities.

Mander told him he need not go into further details on that matter.

I know that photographs of that sort exist. I have seen men gathered in smirking groups looking at them but have never looked myself. Who are the creatures who allow themselves to be photographed in this way? Surely it's impossible to retain any coherent sense of self after submitting to that, after photographing that, after looking? Their purpose is arousal, but self-disgust must follow. I stared at the man in the dock: his brushed hair, unsmiling mouth, firm nose, handsome jaw — and although he looked straight ahead, never flinched, never blinked, saw him change into something without outline or shape. Not some lewd, unhealthy thing. It was more horrible than that. Into nothing. I turned my eyes away. I could not look at him.

❧

The hearing had only a short time to run. It was over by mid-afternoon. Joll's lawyer, Wybrow — the man who had defended Mrs Maxey — asked scarcely a question.

Two days before, Inspector James Teague had met him and his client at the gaol and handed him a statement taken from Owen Moody at the Wellington Hospital. He told Wybrow that he might, if he wished, allow Joll to read it. The pair retired for twenty minutes. When they returned, Joll told Teague that he had read the statement and made the following endorsement: 'So far as it relates to my own act and deed I admit the above statement to be substantially true. Oliver Joll.'

I don't 'remember' the man who read it to the court. I can picture him if I try (it was Teague), but the person I see is Owen Moody and the voice I hear is his.

Here's the full text. It's rather stilted. I remember thinking, He writes better fiction than fact.

'I am an accounts clerk, twenty-nine years of age, and reside at Oriental Bay, Wellington. I met Mr Joll on Saturday the 17th of August while attending a football match in Lower Hutt. I had read his name in newspapers and knew he was a former City Councillor and a parliamentary candidate. I knew nothing of his occupation as a manufacturer. We got on spendidly and talked of many things. When Mr Joll invited me and a friend to have dinner with him on the following Monday night at the St George Hotel we had no hesitation in accepting.'

(The *Dominion* report, which I'm using, is printed in solid blocks. I'm going to put it into paragraphs and drop the sub-headings: A Discovery in Joll's Office; A Pistol Fired, etc.)

'Nothing out of the ordinary happened while at dinner. Mr Joll was a friendly host. Our conversation included cricket, the cinema, politics, on which we agreed, Mr Joll's business, detective stories and Western stories, where our tastes coincided, and many other things. I found Mr Joll to be good company and invited him to have dinner with me, at the St George Hotel again, later in the week. He accepted. I admit that it was my plan to approach him about employment at this meeting as I saw no possibility of advancement where I was.

'We met on Friday the 23rd and had a friendly and enjoyable dinner. I brought up the subject of employment and Mr Joll seemed pleased. He said that he had been looking for "a bright young chap with experience" and that I might "fit the bill". He asked me to call on him at his office the following week to discuss the matter.

'Before that date I ran into Mr Joll in the street and went with him for lunch at his club. I had finished my employment with Barnhill Importers after an argument with the head clerk. When I told Mr Joll, he was amused. He said I had burned my boats but he liked a young fellow with spirit. He invited me to his office, where he offered me a glass of whisky. Although I don't like whisky, I drank it. The question of a job never came up but he reminded me as I left that we had an appointment to talk about it later in the week.

'On Thursday, at about half past one, I again ran into Mr Joll in the street. He was coming back from lunch and invited me into a hotel for a glass of beer. I began to wonder if it was sensible to be on such familiar terms with a man who might become my employer.

'We went to his office at two o'clock. There I discovered a certain disgusting feature in Mr Joll's character. He took an envelope from his safe and showed me several photographs of nude women. From comments he made I began to suspect that his interests lay elsewhere, so I purposely encouraged him to display those qualities of his nature I expected. Mr Joll showed me photographs of nude men.

'I understood that he had dirty intentions. For a short while I led him on in order to be sure. Then I told him that his behaviour disgusted me. I was angry to have been subjected to advances of such a foul nature and raised my voice several times as I denounced him. Mr Joll appeared shocked. Later he attempted to bluster. He claimed that he had been joking, then that he had just been making sure that I was a healthy-minded young fellow. None of this had any effect on me. The photographs he had shown and certain remarks he had made had convinced me of his perverted nature.

'I then told Mr Joll that he was not a fit person to be a member of Parliament and that he must resign as a candidate in the election to be held later this year.'

I've had to take a break in my transcription — cannot stand the bad air that seems to fill my study. I walked in the garden, where Rose joined me. She saw that I was troubled and asked me what it was. I haven't told her of the task I've set myself — have told no one. I do not want to spread the contagion.

I said that a piece of writing I was engaged on was giving me trouble — not a leader for the *Dominion*, I told her (I've given that up, not feeling that I can any longer judge and pronounce), but an historical thing that was leading me into places where I did not want to go. Rose understands me: knows when I want her to ask questions and when not. She led me round the garden, showed me plants and flowers, then stopped at the bank we've let run wild. Nasturtiums have taken it over. Their glorious red flowers floated like coracles on a sea of green. Last night's rain had left water drops the size of pearls cupped in the leaves. I thought I had never seen anything so pure. 'You could drink it,' Rose said, tipping one into her palm. It lost its shape. 'Oh, how sad. I wanted to swallow it whole.' She licked it off, then laughed at her silliness; but to me she personified beauty and good health and I began to feel again the greater weight of good than evil in the world. I knew that I had the strength to describe those things I've set myself to face for a second time and, indeed, that they are less terrible than they appear in the night when I lie awake . . .

I'll hold the memory of my wife in the garden, I'll see the pearl of water in the leaf, and go on until I reach the end . . .

'He pleaded for mercy. He begged me not to force him to resign, saying that he would never be able to explain it to his wife. He made me look at a photograph of his wife and daughters. Such hypocrisy disgusted me further and I told him to put his other photographs away before showing me his family. I was, however, anxious to be just and do nothing cruel to innocent people, so I allowed Mr Joll to explain himself.

'He told me he was suffering from a complaint that made it impossible for him to control his passions. His doctor would satisfy me in that respect. He rang up his doctor but could not get through.

'Mr Joll became very earnest. He asked me to allow him several days to put his affairs in order and then he would kill himself. I did not believe him. It seemed to me that he was trying to give himself time to arrange some means of denying what had taken place in his office. By now I was thoroughly done up with the strain of the conversation. I was terribly tired and wanted to get away. I told him I would give him one day but that he should not think of suicide, rather of some convincing way of telling his decision to his wife. I repeated that he had no business in Parliament. My concern was that he should not be in public life,

147

where his pretence of being normal would be corrupting in itself.

'Mr Joll laughed at me, which was astonishing. He said he liked me as a man and that we should put the last hour aside — bury the whole steaming mess was the expression he used — and get on with our lives as men of the world. He told me he would give me a job at whatever rate of pay I cared to name.

'I became very angry at this. I was deeply insulted and my desire to leave Mr Joll's company became intense. I told him I would call on him the next day to discuss the form his resignation would take, but in the meantime I must have a note promising that he would resign a week from that day for reasons of unstable mental health. It must be addressed to me at the General Post Office, and registered. I said it would lie there until his resignation was complete. Then I would hand it back to him.

'After further argument Mr Joll agreed. I dictated the letter, which he signed. I sealed it in an envelope and we took it downstairs to the office girl and told her to take it to the post office at once. While waiting for her to come back with the receipt, I went upstairs with Mr Joll again. This was a mistake. I was forced to listen to further pleading, then to his attempt to justify his appetites. I told him to be silent. When the office girl returned I went downstairs, took the receipt and went home.

'I felt drained of energy and thoroughly worn out. My encounter with Mr Joll — the Joll behind his public face — was the most unpleasant experience of my life.'

Owen Moody goes on: 'Before calling on Mr Joll the following afternoon I went to the post office and took delivery of the registered letter. Although I had told him I would let it lie for a week, I was afraid he might find some way of getting hold of it. I believed it would be safer in my possession. During my final talk with Mr Joll it remained in my pocket.

'I understand that this letter has never been found. I can only suppose that it fell out during our struggle, or when I was being cared for downstairs, or that some person removed it from my clothes at the hospital. I have no knowledge of its present whereabouts.

'In Mr Joll's office on Friday the 30th of August, the conversation of the previous day repeated itself. Mr Joll implored me for a month's time and spoke again about his wife and family. I remained firm. I said that he must resign that afternoon and explained that I was letting him off lightly. By rights his true nature should be exposed.

'Mr Joll changed his tack and refused to resign. He claimed that he had not yet talked to his wife. I told him that he must do the best he could, and that I was going to take his letter to the newspaper and explain the circumstances under which it had been written. I turned to leave. I heard Mr Joll open a drawer. He called out my name.

'When I turned I saw that he had a pistol pointing at my chest.

'He said, "This is for you," and fired immediately.

'I felt the bullet enter my chest and I fell down. Mr Joll came round his desk and looked at me. He thrust the pistol into my right hand. Then he ran out of the office.

'I climbed to my feet, holding the pistol. I seized a chair from in front of the desk and smashed the glass in the window over Taranaki Street. I threw the chair out and called to some chaps in the street that I had been shot.

'Mr Joll came back into the office. He cried out, "For God's sake shoot me, Owen." I attempted to keep his desk between us while keeping him covered. He rushed at me and tried to take the pistol. I kept it pointing away and let off all the shots until it was empty.

'I don't remember much more. I heard Mr Joll say that I had shot myself by accident. There were many people looking down at me. One of them, a young woman I thought very pretty, tried to give me first aid. I lost consciousness and did not recover until many hours later in the hospital.'

Teague then read Joll's endorsement admitting that the description of his acts and deeds was substantially true.

Oliver Joll as I picture him: he shifts, I lose him, I see this part and that; strong neck, wide shoulders, chest and stomach of a well-fed man; face with its confidence gone — social, joking, dining, deciding confidence — but in its place a resignation contented with itself, with knowledge gained and expectation put aside. His cheeks and mouth and jowls retain their carved fleshiness but there's a skin taken off. His eyes have a colour more subdued than their former blue. I detest the man. I admire him too — but only in this manifestation: he stands and folds his arms, and answers the clerk's question in his firm and normal voice: 'I plead guilty.'

Rose said, 'Do you have to go today? It's not doing you any good, Sam.'

She was right. It was harming me. It was taking one of *my* skins away and making an impression like badly inked print on the nervous membrane underneath. Nothing can be trusted, I found there. There are hideous places one must look, and so on.

I said goodbye to her and walked down to the Supreme Court. Outside I met Eric. He had sailed up from Christchurch in the night on the *Rangatira* — was tousled in his hair, misbuttoned in his waistcoat, shaved in a haphazard way. I hailed him, felt my voice come back.

'Poor devil,' Eric said when the court guards brought Joll in for sentencing.

Wybrow, who had been short of questions the day before, was full of words that morning. He pattered them like rain, firm one moment, hushed the next, trying in his professional way to wash Joll clean in the steady fall. There's no telling with the Chief Justice (Sir Michael Green). He has a way of being neutral while looking keen; and a way, then, of indicating in a word or gesture that although argument flows on, the rock of justice lying underneath will not be changed. (I wrote that several years ago in an article on Sir Michael, trying to suggest his Jewishness, and it still seems true.) He gave Wybrow all the time he needed, interjecting only two or three times: 'We understand the weight of it,' when Wybrow went on a little too long about the heavy responsibility he and his friend McMurtry bore in advising the accused to plead guilty. They had hesitated a long while but decided in the end that it was the only honourable course. It was not clear to me whether he meant for Joll or for themselves.

More careful then, but wordy still, Wybrow continued: 'Your Honour, it is part of my duty, which I willingly accept, to exonerate the unfortunate young man, Moody, from all blame in this matter. I fully acknowledge that no responsibility whatsoever can be attached to him for the dreadful events that occurred in the accused's office. They do not reflect on his character in the slightest way. Mr Moody's action must meet with the commendation of all right-thinking men. I say this with the full concurrence and approval of the accused.'

'Who does he think he's representing?' Eric whispered.

I looked at Joll. His eyes seemed thoughtful but unconcerned. He was gone from the day and the proceedings. He's absent, I thought. All this is happening without him.

Wybrow came back to his business. The accused, he said, was a man of considerable attainments. He had worked his way up from humble beginnings, had done sufficiently well at school to have continued his education at the university, had he wished, and perhaps entered one of the professions, but he chose instead to go into business and make his mark there. He had been a member of the Territorial Army, had been an early volunteer in the Great War, where he rose to the rank of First Lieutenant. He was mentioned in dispatches for an act of extraordinary gallantry at Messines. The pistol used in the shooting was a souvenir of that war. The accused had kept it in his office for protection in these uncertain times. That was unfortunate but many men in his financial position would do the same.

'You must not excuse illegalities, Mr Wybrow,' Sir Michael said.

'No Your Honour, it's not my intention.' Wybrow took a sip of water, then looked into his glass as though he might find a drowned fly there. Yet he had good things left to say about Joll: he ran his business efficiently, and with honesty — ask any man who had dealt with him. His career in local body politics was notable and his ambition to higher office a matter of record. He might soon have occupied an important position, one of the most honourable his fellow citizens could bestow.

Wybrow sipped again. He had come to the matter he did not wish to discuss. Reluctance hampered his wordiness, but after a stumble he managed both precision and reserve.

'Now — I scarcely know what to say.'

'Take your time, Mr Wybrow.'

'Your Honour — he finds himself in this position, facing this charge. It's a matter for deep concern and regret. I draw Your Honour's attention to the underlying cause in justification of the accused and in the hope of mitigating the sentence to be passed.' Wybrow wiped his mouth with his handkerchief — perhaps to wipe away 'justification', for there was none.

'Your Honour, inquiries have been made. And it has been found that for a number of years the accused has been suffering from homosexual monomania. I have gone into the matter considerably with him and believe I am justified in speaking of the efforts he has made to cure himself. He has consulted doctors and meta-physicians. I have statements here from one of the doctors and one of the metaphysicians, and both attest to the accused's deep distress at his condition and the strenuous efforts he has made to return himself to a normal state.'

Wybrow handed the statements to Sir Michael, who glanced at them and put them aside. He nodded at Wybrow to continue.

'Your Honour, for some months the accused has been suffering from overwork and mental strain. He has been attempting to expand his business while at the same time taking important steps to increase his involvement in public life. There has also been his constant deep-seated worry about his medical condition. All these matters, along with the sudden threat of exposure and consequent ruin, the pain and disgrace to his family, the loss of his ambitions and the opportunity to serve his community and country — these things, Your Honour, drove him to extremities and unhinged his mind, with the results that have been described.

'I ask you to take them into account and in your judgement temper justice with mercy.'

Sir Michael thanked him. The court rose for half an hour to give him time to read the documents handed to him.

We did not stray far from the court. There was a great curiosity to see Joll sentenced and we did not wish to risk losing our seats.

'He's a lucky man,' Dudley Aimer said.

'What do you mean?'

'Just half an inch the other way and he'd have been hanged.'

'He might have got away with his story,' Eric said.

'An accident? With a bullet in the middle of the chest? Who'd buy that?'

'Young Moody's the sort of man to play with a loaded gun.'

'I wish I could see him. Is he some sort of pretty boy? A Valentino?'

'No, he's not. He's a damn fool, though, trying to beat down a man like Joll. Why couldn't he let it lie? Just get out of there instead of stirring up muck?'

'And let Joll get into Parliament?' I said, astonished.

'Yes, yes, we all know what you think,' Eric said. 'Ah, it's time. Let's go and see justice done.'

Sir Michael dispensed it without drama. His tone was regretful more than condemnatory. I could not help thinking, He's a Jew, there are centuries and histories behind him.

Joll faced him with folded arms. I imagined that a beam of recognition passed between them. I don't mean of a sexual sort, God forbid, or of acquaintanceship, for they were acquainted, but of (I put it as simply as I can) human understanding. Joll was neither defiant nor accepting. He was resigned. He was, if I don't mistake it, faintly amused. I've no doubt he suffered agonies, and suffers them still, but this moment, his sentencing, this ending of his life in the world, interested him. He gave it a small nod of greeting.

Sir Michael, speaking evenly, as though giving advice, told him he was sorry to see him in this position. Told him his career in business had been successful and his behaviour exemplary, as far as was known. His contributions to public life had been useful, while his ambition to serve in a higher political sphere was, Sir Michael accepted, honest and without taint. He might have gone far. He might have had a brilliant career. Instead he found himself here, in the dock, facing a most serious charge.

'Your attempt at murder was an impulsive act. Mr Moody's statement indicates that, and these statements from the doctor and the person describing himself as a metaphysician show that you have made more than one attempt to find a cure for the condition — which cannot, however, be described as medical — that afflicts you. I take that into account.

'I hope that you will redeem yourself. You have taken a first step in that direction by pleading guilty.

'I have been asked to pass sentence with compassion and mercy. But the ideal of justice is that human life is sacred, otherwise the community is doomed.'

Sir Michael pushed his notes aside. He sentenced Oliver Joll to fifteen years' imprisonment with hard labour.

Ten

He vanished from sight and will fade from memory. I have taken on, unwillingly, the job of preserving him, in order that, in some future time, others may look at him floating in my jar, in my solution, *Oliver Joll*, and say, Yes, interesting, poor chap, what a tragedy, what a waste of talents, what darkness there, what an ugly worm feeding inside — all of that, which I'll accept, and say, I've done my job, what you make of him is up to you. I think and feel the way I must.

Now I have a further job: to look at the others. I am equally unwilling for that.

Early October. Joll is gone. His wife has changed her name and shifted to another town. New entertainments carry us along: Jeanette Macdonald and Nelson Eddy in *Naughty Marietta*; Noel Coward in *The Scoundrel*. The Mareo case in Auckland shunts the Joll case further into the distance down the line. Mussolini launches his war on Abyssinia, and a thousand policemen fail to control fighting between negroes and Italians in Harlem. In Wellington, Viscount Galway opens the Academy of Fine Arts exhibition in the Whitmore Street Gallery and detects the emergence of a New Zealand school — 'artists who have not had the opportunity of receiving tuition in the Old Land'. Charlie has two watercolours in but no one buys them. Harold Fine calls them 'more pleasing than is usual for this artist' in his review.

I said to Eric, 'How is she getting on out there? Have you seen her?'

'She's housekeeping. She's washing James's socks and ironing his shirts.'

'What about Mrs Hearn?'

'She's sacked. Ferrabee couldn't get on with her.'

The following day a deputation of Melling members of the National Political League (the old Coalition) waited on James. He consented to be the party's official candidate in the November elections.

He tried to avoid the hustings. He meant to be voted in because he was James Tinling. His record would speak for him, while his natural gift of — let's call it superiority — stood him out from his Labour opponent like a racehorse from a donkey pulling a cart. (I've stolen that from Dudley Aimer's cartoon, which showed the donkey patient and sturdy, while John Citizen examined the horse's teeth.)

At those meetings he could not avoid, James abandoned his bogus vulgarity. He stood in a long and honourable tradition of service (by which he meant, but did not say, *noblesse oblige*), of rectitude and head-down honest work for a fair reward, and, where all else failed, the helping hand. The helping hand must never become a principle of policy, or the foundations of civil government would fail and that noble structure, the ordered society, fall into the morass of socialism.

'He said that?' Eric asked me, amazed.

'It says so here.'

'Let's go and hear him.'

Rose would not come. It was 'too soon after Violet' for James to see his family 'goggling at him fishy eyed'. May could not. She had taken on, at short notice, the job of secretary to the Women's Welfare League and was swamped with work.

Eric and I drove out to the Hutt without our wives. It was a cool spring night with a clear sky and a full moon.

'Earth's crystal paramour,' Eric said.

'Yes, don't tell me.' Shelley again.

We were late arriving and the meeting had begun. A dozen cars were parked outside the hall, James's among them, with Lennie Ferrabee sitting at ease on the running-board. He rolled a cigarette as we approached.

'Evening, gents,' he said, after licking it.

'Shouldn't you be inside supporting your boss?'

'I hear enough of him at home. Did you see what happened to my old boss, eh? I always thought he smelled of oh dee colognee. I wonder how he'll get on cracking rocks.' He grinned wide-mouthed, with monkey cheeks; stood up from the running-board and took his matches out. 'Charlotte couldn't come tonight. She's got a headache.'

'Listen, Ferrabee,' I began.

'Lennie, not Ferrabee, Mr Holloway.'

'Lennie,' Eric said, 'I'll tell you something, free advice. Keep away from Miss Tinling. If I hear one more time that you've been pestering her . . .'

'She's got her old man looking after her.'

'One more time, I'll come out and teach you a lesson you won't forget.'

'You think you could do that?'

'Oh yes.' Eric grinned at him. 'And I think you know it.'

I pulled his arm. 'Come on. Don't even talk to him.' Ferrabee looked ready to fight. I had the impression he would be deadly: that he would bait Eric like a bear and leave him, bleeding, half a turn behind. I pulled him again.

Ferrabee laughed and lit his cigarette. 'You've got a good second there, Prof.' He flicked his burning match over our heads.

'Come on.' We went along to the hall entrance. 'What's he been doing with Charlie?'

Eric made a sound of disgust. 'Remarks that can mean one thing or the other. You know, he's smart. "I wouldn't wear that dress, Miss Tinling." Meaning, It doesn't suit you, or maybe, Take it off for me, darlin', OK?'

'Does she tell James?'

'She's tried once or twice. James said something to him but he doesn't stop. I'll go out there. I wasn't kidding.'

In the hall, we found the simmer of good fellowship that precedes uproar. Melling is a mixed electorate. It runs south into Petone, taking in factory workers, many of them unemployed, and over to Hutt, where Walter Nash was (still is) the member, but includes pockets of the well-to-do, enough to make it marginal. James had been its member until his loss two elections before. He must have thought his constituents had recognised their mistake — how else explain his confidence?

Douglas Drake was the Labour candidate. There was also Clive Gleeson, a Social Crediter, and Toby Small, a Democrat. Small was finishing as we went in. We might have been listening to James. The Democrats were the broken bits of Campbell Begg's New Zealand Legion, old Reform Party men, sheep farmers with anarchist tendencies, businessmen who wanted no state theft of 'the blood of our endeavour and bone of our hard work', as Toby Small, his fists pumping, declared in his peroration.

'Don't give us that manure,' cried a jokester near the back.

We found a place beside the door as hoots of laughter reddened Small's face.

'Next,' cried the men. 'Give us little Duggie, Duggie Duck.'

First they had to listen to the Social Crediter, and then they had to listen to James.

He began, 'Well, ladies and gentlemen, you know me.'

· 'No we don't. Who are you? You're Gordon Coates's shoe-shine boy. You're the so-and-so that eats the cake while our kids don't even get any bread,' and so on.

'Well, he asked for it. He used to be good at reading meetings,' Eric said.

James made no step back, no appeal to the chairman. Had he seen that there were votes he would never get, voters he need not waste argument on, and that his supporters would want him measured and calm and above the fray, *virtute securus*? His eyes found them here and there, picked them out and sent them the message of his demeanour; and when the hall was quiet enough, he went on: 'You know me, gentlemen, for a man who tells the truth, no matter what company he finds himself in.'

He waited out the uproar again. He took his watch from his fob pocket — offensive in itself, a watch like that — and calmly wound it; and it seemed crazy to me, for there must be working men in the hall who would vote for him from that old ineradicable conservatism they carry in them like a ganglion on a nerve. James was saying, I'm not here to talk to you, you don't count. I've never seen a worse political performance. Yet there was good politics in it too, if you count the way he made his hecklers perform for the voters he was only partly sure of. Had he studied them as Small and Gleeson spoke, and seen that he could frighten them with a mob and secure them with James Tinling, gentleman?

He used only ten minutes of his allotted twenty. I had never heard his voice so sharp and thin. It cut like a chisel, stabbed with dismissive epithets and kept a sawmill buzz at the edge. These are the facts, he said; and, I am untouchable, seemed to say. When he spoke to the workmen it was not only to them, for he sent a message over their heads, by some sleight of intonation, to those who would agree that uneducated men could not hope to understand the ways in which money works and countries are run.

'I'll keep it simple,' James said at the end. 'The Labour Party makes all this noise about "using the public credit" and "issuing sufficient money to meet the needs of the nation". This is bush economics, my friends. All it will do is create worthless paper money. You'll see it fluttering in the streets and not even bother to pick it up. Five pounds will not be worth five pence. It's printing-press money. They are ignorant men you propose to follow. They're from Australia, most of them, aren't they? And they come to you with their talk of creating credit and putting up your wages and starting pension schemes, while they haven't the slightest notion of what it means. They think they'll sit in their brand-new offices and sign bits of paper and it's done. What folly. They'll be signing for higher taxes, that's all. They'll be signing your future out of existence. They'll be bringing down the institutions that genera-tions of honest men, generations of hard-working New Zealanders have built up by the sweat of their brow. They'll wreck the banks you've put your savings in —'

'What savings?' the men cried.

Indeed, what savings? How had James got so out of touch? He waited for the shouting to subside, then said, 'I've told you what I think and I won't say any more, except this: If you want the evils of a foreign creed, if you want economic ruin and monetary disease and a country that's no more than a heap of bones, you'll vote for

164

the man you call Duggie Duck, but if you'd sooner put a vertebral column and a spinal cord into this nation you'll give your vote to James Tinling and the National Political League.'

He went back to his seat, sat down with slow precision and became as absent from proceedings as Oliver Joll had been from his sentencing.

'Duggie, Little Duggie, Duggie Duck,' supporters cried, as the squat little fellow stepped out. Instead of stopping midway between the table and the front of the stage, he went right to the edge, overlapped it with his toes, bent and put his hands on his knees, and said, 'Fellow workers, you know me.'

They whistled and cheered, while the backs of James's supporters stiffened with indignation or contracted with sudden fear.

'I'm the man who'll tell you how this government of lawyers and fat farmers and their stooges has put its boot on you and kept it there for the last ten years — longer than that, since the war. How they've herded you like cattle into camps, with their stock-whips cracking.' (Drake grew up in Australia.) 'You know the places I'm talking about. Aka Aka, up the valley, eh? How many of you have been there? Yes, so have I, and got callouses on my hands to show for it, while they get — these Reform and Liberal fellows, yes that's their name, it's a new hat they're wearing but the same old face underneath — they get their callouses on their bums from their office chairs.'

The chairman called for order. He asked Drake to keep his language clean, which made the little fellow thin himself with astonishment. He's got a clown's face, Douglas Drake, it's India rubber, and the timing of a vaudeville comedian. He mimed contrition. He pulled out his handkerchief and scrubbed the dirty word off his lips.

'On their posteriors,' he said, la-di-da.

It was entertainment as much as politics. Eric held his laughter in beside me. 'I think he's been sent to punish James.'

'He's been sent to convince him that he'll win.' I meant that he underlined who was the gentleman.

Drake used his full twenty minutes. Behind the entertainer there's a politician who never misses a trick. 'You know, my friends,' he said at the end, 'I read a bit of poetry. Yes, I do. I can see that surprises some of my fellow countrymen in the audience. They don't think poetry is for working men. Well, they're wrong, and here's a bit. It's from Shelley. You've all heard of Shelley. Got run out of England, he did, for daring to speak his mind. It's a song to the men of England, but I reckon it does for New Zealand just as well. Listen:

> *Men of England, wherefore plough*
> *For the lords who lay ye low?*
> *Wherefore weave with toil and care*
> *The rich robes your tyrants wear?*

> *Wherefore feed, and clothe, and save,*
> *From the cradle to the grave,*
> *Those ungrateful drones who would*
> *Drain your sweat — nay, drink your blood?'*

I was less surprised by his choice (politician, I called him a moment ago, but he can also be a rabble-rouser) than by Eric's reaction.

'Bravo!' he cried. He clapped his hands.

Drake grinned at him. 'We've even got a professor on our side.'

James closed his eyes. He turned his head a fraction, opened them, held Eric in his gaze, then, I think, subtracted him from his world of certainties and concerns, made Eric cease to be, and me as well; signalled it by uncrossing his legs and recrossing them the other way. He took out his handkerchief, patted his mouth, folded it along its lines and slid it neatly back in his breast pocket. He can, by doing small things precisely, terrify.

Eric gave Drake a wag of his finger. He turned to me: 'Had enough?'

We left the hall.

'You've finished us with James,' I said.

'I was finished already.'

We passed James's car, with Ferrabee behind the wheel in the dark. His eyes caught light as he turned his head. They glinted at us.

'I'm glad I'm not in this electorate,' I said.

'Who would you vote for?'

'Not Small. Not James either.'

'I'd vote for Shelley. Hey —' he increased his pace — 'look at this. The little bugger.' The two front tyres of his car were flat. 'That's Ferrabee. I'll wring his neck.'

'No, Eric —'

'Who else could it be?'

'They might be punctures.'

'Both of them?' Then Eric laughed. 'All right. We won't give him the satisfaction.' He crouched and looked at the nearer tyre. 'Jammed a match stick in the valve, see?' He took the match out and tossed it away, then took off his jacket and threw it on the bonnet. 'Exercise, my boy. Get your coat off.'

He fetched the jack and pump from the boot and passed from annoyance to satisfaction, lying down and fitting the jack, then to a kind of measuring interest in the working of his arm and the lifting of the car. He loosened the nuts holding the wheel, jacked again, gave them a twist with his fingers, placed them on the bonnet by our coats, then lifted the wheel off and laid it on the footpath. Sweat shone on his forehead. He wiped it with his sleeve.

'Have a go at that with the pump.'

I coupled it, stood it on the pavement, set my hands and feet, and went to work, while three cars down the line Ferrabee watched from behind the wheel of James's Austin. He lit a cigarette. His face was printed yellow then sank into the dark.

Eric brought the spare tyre from the boot. He bounced it on the road, hoisted it and lowered it three or four times over his head.

'Let's see little Lennie do that.' He fitted the wheel, screwed on the nuts, tightened them. 'How's it going with that one, Sam?'

I was panting. My hands were burning. I wanted to rest but did not want Ferrabee to see.

Eric lowered the jack and gave the nuts a final jerk with the wrench. 'It's a bit soft but it'll get us home.' He shifted round to the far side of the car and lay on the road.

The hall made a rumbling cough, a clearing of its throat, as the audience — men, I almost wrote, but there were women too — poured out. I used their flowing by as a reason to stop pumping. Wound my handkerchief round my palm.

'Puncture, matey?' said a man.

'No, someone let our tyres down.'

Douglas Drake stopped in a group. 'That's politics for you.'

Eric's face rose like a moon over the bonnet. 'It was personal.'

'Let's lend a hand,' Drake said. He took the pump from where I had let it fall and set to work. The car rose on the other side as Eric jacked. Perhaps it was exhaustion: the night began to seem unreal. Along the road James paused by the door of his car. Ferrabee leaned across the seat and opened it. I thought, The world is changing, you can feel the breath of it, we're in a new time.

Drake took off his jacket and handed it to one of his friends. He spat on his hands and fell to pumping again. Ferrabee drove away, with James staring ahead.

'Tin lung,' shouted the men waiting by Eric's car.

'Go easy on him, boys, he's an old man,' Drake said. 'Jump on that, Jackie, and see if it's tight.'

One of the men stood on the tyre. 'She'll do.'

Drake carried it round to Eric, who lifted the second wheel off.

'I'll put a bit more air in this,' the man called Jackie said. He fastened the pump to the tyre Eric had changed and set to work. Eric and Drake fitted the wheel on the other side and tightened the nuts. I took my tobacco pouch from my coat and filled my pipe. I was light headed from my unaccustomed work, and from overturning Ferrabee and defeating James. Was that what we had done, defeated him? The notion was in keeping with my heightened sense of the night, of our pocket of good fellowship in the enclosing streets, and Eric and Drake instructing each other as they worked.

As if returning things to their mundane state, the car slumped level on its wheels.

I lit my pipe and smoked while Jackie and two others took turns in pumping the last tyre. Eric reached into the glovebox for a packet of tailor-mades. He offered them round. Then he and Drake exchanged bits of Shelley — 'Man who man would be, Must rule the empire of himself...' — until each was satisfied. Drake shook hands and walked off with his cohort to 'whet our whistles down at Jackie's place'. Their hats shone under the streetlamps; their laughter rang off fences along the street. James can't see them, I thought. He hasn't the faintest notion where they came from or where they're going.

Eric started the car and we drove home.

'Sore hands?' he asked.

'I'm all right. It was Ferrabee who let them down. James wouldn't stoop.'

'Maybe. I'd like to know one thing, though. What's he keeping on a thug like Ferrabee for?'

Eleven

I picked up a chill from sweating and Rose kept me inside for the rest of the week. I spent the time writing to the surviving members of our murder story group, explaining that I would not be carrying on as editor, or as contributor either, offering those who wanted them their chapters back, and suggesting that they get together and restart the novel, or a similar or a different one, if they were inclined. I did not expect them to be.

I had not heard from Owen Moody since the shooting. Addressing me as 'Sam', he wrote: 'You can keep my chapter as a souvenir. It got me thinking about what I should do, so it wasn't wasted. What a load of codswallop, though, a bunch of old hacks — and young ones too (self excluded) — setting up as Agatha Christie. I won't be playing that sort of game again.

'You ask about my health. Do you mean the bullet? It'll take more than that to finish me. Joll caught me by surprise with that pistol but what's the use of using it if you can't shoot straight? Now I'm off to the Old Country. I'm sailing on the *Ionic* the week after next and I don't intend coming back. Why spend your life in the bottom half of the world? O. M.'

The bullet hadn't damaged his conceit.

I was sitting in the summerhouse on a mild afternoon, reading one of my favourites, Georgette Heyer, and learning how to make characters move and a story flow — I thought I might write my own light novel but turn her Regency heiresses and beaux into departmental clerks and D.I.C. shopgirls — when I heard the gate open and saw Freddie and Elsie on the path. I considered hiding, then called them over to spare Rose.

They had been to visit Eric and May but not found them home, so had brought themselves down the hill to Rose and me. Elsie, mottled from walking, fanned her chest with her blouse, while Freddie took his jacket off and adjusted from city gent to man at ease in his family. He mopped his face.

'A drink would go down well,' he said.

'Something cold?'

'Tea,' Elsie said. 'Beer makes Freddie belch.'

'It's my indigestion,' he protested.

I left them disputing — she butting on, he giving ground — and asked Rose to bring out a tray.

'What do they want?'

'No idea. Elsie's got her bull-at-a-gate look.'

'And Freddie's rubbing round her like a moggy, I suppose.'

I took out a bottle of beer for myself.

'We really wanted Eric's advice,' Elsie said as I sat down.

'But I'll do?'

'Is Rose coming out? No offence, but she and May and Eric —'

'The sensible ones?' I was lumped in with Freddie. 'Doesn't it strike you that a lifetime working on newspapers . . . Ah, never mind. What's Taylor done this time?'

'How did you know it was him?'

'It usually is.'

'He hasn't done anything bad, Sam,' Freddie said.

'Just something stupid?'

'If you have to be rude we'll go somewhere else,' Elsie said, her redness flaring.

I apologised, and asked them, as civilly as I could, what the matter was.

'He borrowed money off Freddie. Borrowed, that's a laugh. And made him promise not to tell me.'

'Broke my promise,' Freddie joked, apologetically.

'I knew when I saw the ticket who must have paid.'

'What ticket?'

'For the boat. He's going to England. He and that friend of his, Owen Moody. He's too young, Sam.'

'And he's got no job,' Freddie said.

'No job he can do, except working behind a counter, which I don't have to tell you was a huge disappointment to us.'

'He spends all his money,' Freddie said.

'He can't save.'

'But he sold his motorbike, Elsie, remember that.'

'Pooh. Twenty pounds. And that's all gone. I know what will happen when the pair of them get to London. They'll be sending back home to us for money.'

'I'm not worried about that. It's what might happen to him.' Freddie turned his head to hide tears in his eyes.

'It's the wrong time to be gallivanting round the world,' Elsie said.

'He's nineteen,' Freddie said.

'And that Moody's the sort of man who could get him into trouble.'

'A man who's been shot,' Freddie said.

'That wasn't his fault. But he's a smart alec. And he's got no job either. The pair of them could starve. Taylor just laughs when I say that.'

Rose brought the tray out and poured tea. Elsie repeated her complaint.

'It's no use asking us,' Rose said. 'Taylor will go his own way. There's more to him than you think, Elsie. He'll survive.'

'That's easy for you to say with your two married and gone.'

'I think he'll bounce up like a rubber ball.'

'What we wanted —' Freddie began.

'All we need to know,' Elsie said, 'is if you think we should stop him. Which we can do. Because he's still under twenty-one. He'd be upset —'

'I can imagine,' Rose said.

'— but he'd thank us in the end.'

'No,' Rose said.

'No, what?'

'Don't stop him. If you want my advice —'

'Sam, what do you think?'

'He'd find some way of sneaking on board. I'd let him go. Moody's not a bad chap. He'll keep an eye on him. And when they run out of money they can work their passage home. Plenty of young chaps do that.'

'Yes, but . . .' Elsie went round again. When she had finished and we'd softened our advice (while keeping it the same) Rose took her into the house. I rinsed my glass at the garden tap and poured Freddie the last of the beer.

'Stand up for yourself, Freddie.'

'I can't. I've tried. She runs right over the top of me. I'm not complaining. We're happy in our way.' He tried to grin. 'Even if it's not much of a way. You've no idea . . .'

I waited.

'You've no idea what having Taylor meant to me. Having a son. As long as he was all right I was all right, I didn't mind. But when he went into his own place ...'

'What is it, Freddie?'

'With Owen Moody ... Sam, do you think there's maybe something unhealthy there?'

I felt the tiny jolt of mind that comes when one glimpses, then loses sight of, the insupportable. 'No, Freddie, no. Moody's all right. He's a funny sort of codger, that's easy to see. And conceited. And selfish. Arrogant too. But look how he put Joll's weights up as soon as he found out what he was like. If anything, he'll be a good influence on Taylor. Stop him playing silly games, I mean.'

'You think — Taylor's all right?'

'Yes, he is. He is. He likes to pose a bit, that's all. He's young. He plays football, Freddie. I've seen him score tries.'

'And Moody plays cricket.'

'They're just a couple of young chaps feeling their oats. Let him go away. He'll be grown up when he comes back. You won't know him.'

I helped him wrap up his suspicions and put them in some back corner of his mind, where I hope they'll stay. I had never dreamed of his great love for his son. But now I harboured something that kept out of sight, moving each time I turned my head.

I repeated to myself what I'd said to Freddie: he'll be all right, he's young, he plays the fool. That forced opinion stayed in the forefront, hiding just sufficiently the thing I would not see.

Eric telephoned the following day. 'Come to the wrestling, Sam. It's Ken Kenneth versus Bronco Nagurski. I've got the tickets.'

'I can't. I'm still sneezing. I'll get another dose.'

'Wrap yourself up. Kenneth's your man, isn't he? I'm for Nagurski. I hate going to these things by myself.'

He called for me at half past seven in his car.

'Wrong way,' I said as he turned up Hill Street instead of heading for town. He pulled over to the side of the road.

'First off, I'll say I'm sorry.'

'What for?'

'We're not going to the wrestling. I just said that to get you out of the house.'

'Is it James?' I said, alarmed.

'No. Listen, Sam, I know you're not going to like it. I had a note from Lily Maxey yesterday. She wants to see you and me about — she wouldn't say what. She says she's thought about it and it's something we should know. I'm sorry about the mystery —'

'What can she possibly know that concerns me?'

'That's what we'll find out. She's expecting us.'

'I'm getting out. I'll walk home.'

'Sam —' he grasped my arm, fastened it down — 'Lily's not a fool. If she says she's got to see us, it's important. I'm going. If I find out something you should know . . . ?'

'Come and tell me.'

'I don't think I will.' He let go my arm. 'If you want to know what's in the back room, Sam, you open the door.'

'What room? What door? Does May know you're going to this woman?'

'I'm not "going to her". But I'll tell May if it's any of her business. You coming? If not, jump out.'

I stayed in the car. I calmed myself as well as I was able while he drove along to Tinakori Road. I'll confess to a thrill not wholly of alarm, and resolved to be worldly and practical.

She had bought a cottage up the road from the Hill Street corner: a tidy place in a rubbing-shoulders row.

'She's a widow with private means, don't worry, Sam.'

'So there was a Maxey?'

'Nice chap. A house painter. He sang comic songs. He died in 1919 in the flu.'

'He let her do what she did?'

'She'd given up. She only went back when he died. As boss-lady. He left some cash.'

He opened the gate, climbed the two steps to the door, used the knocker: rat-tat, rat-tat-tat — a sequence that filled me with suspicion. Mrs Maxey, spectral behind lace curtains, crossed the room.

'Eric, come in. Mr Holloway.'

I had expected her to play the lady, to be in a role that denied her past — and perhaps she was: the sturdy housewife. Yet it seemed natural to her as she took and hung our coats inside the door and showed us to chairs and went unbustled to the kitchen to fill the kettle and put it on. Her living room was unexceptionable, even to my eye that looked for mark and stain in cheap furniture and showy ornament. An upright piano stood against one wall. A bookcase of novels, Jane Austen to Charlotte M. Yonge, filled another. I sat discomfited in my easy chair.

'Eric,' she said, coming back, 'you're quite a stranger. Are you busy?'

'Just the usual. How do you like it here, Lily? Settling in?'

So they chatted, while I listened for false notes and sniffed the homely air for drifting sin. The kettle whistled and Eric said, 'Turn it off, Lily. Sam and I had better find out what this business is.'

'All right.' She went to the kitchen, silenced the kettle, came back and settled on the sofa — a woman more dowdy than I remembered, in cardigan, warm stockings, an ordinary dress.

'I suppose you know all about me, Mr Holloway?'

'Well, a little,' I answered, discomfited again.

'You'll have seen my name in the paper a while ago and know what business I was in?'

I nodded, averting my eyes.

'Eric —' turning to him — 'I've thought a good deal about what I'm going to say, and it's mainly because you were willing to stand up in court . . .' She smiled. 'I'm glad they didn't call you. Your reputation would be gone.'

'It's a heavy weight on my back sometimes,' he said.

'You wouldn't be happy without it, dear.' (I resented 'dear' on May's behalf, although it was more prod than pat.) 'Anyway, this thing. I'm breaking one of my rules.' She frowned. 'It's like trying to write a letter with my left hand. Mr Holloway —' she had a way of moving her eyes and catching you — 'I'm not asking you to do anything. It's yours and Eric's — you'll see why. Another thing — I'm not taking any moral stand. It's more . . . dislike.'

'Come on, Lily, spit it out,' Eric said.

She smiled at him drily. 'You might be sorry when I do. Anyway, I keep in touch with one or two girls who worked for me. They have to be giving up the life. I stipulate that for my own protection. Some of them don't try very hard. Last week, last Friday — so I've thought about this —' she counted on her fingers — 'six days, that's how much I have to turn myself the other way.'

'All right, Lily,' Eric said patiently.

'One of them came on a visit and she told me what I'm going to tell you. I won't say any names; you can put them in.'

'We'd hardly know hers,' I protested.

'Or mine, Mr Holloway. I hope you'll manage to forget it. Because, when you leave this room, I haven't told you anything that comes back to me. Is that agreed?'

I was tiring of — I won't say her palaver, it had too serious a tone, but her backing off and hedging. And I resented her cornering of us, of our response, before she had told us anything. We should be in charge, and questioning her, not she choosing what and how to tell. Yet I had no question except, What are you trying to say? It made a hard lump in my throat.

'This girl of mine thought she was getting married, but she was wrong. The man — well, he's not the marrying kind. What he is, though, is the sort of fellow who puffs himself up. He likes to drink and he likes to talk. There's a lot like that. It's amazing what some men will say. This girl —'

'Give her a name, call her Mary,' Eric said.

'All right, Mary. She was furious with him, understandably. But she'll do better. I told her that. There's a lot of my girls have made good wives, Mr Holloway. But some of them think they've got to throw themselves away. This girl wants to get her own back. I've told her it's not a good idea. Just stay away from the man, get as far away as you can, that's what I said.'

'Are you saying he's someone we know?' Eric said.

'I'm not sure. You might have seen him. He used to work for Oliver Joll.'

'And now he works for James Lawrence Tinling, am I right?'

'I've said one name but I'm not saying that.'

'Or Ferrabee? There's nothing he can do.'

'He can give my young girl a hard time. He doesn't seem to care who he hurts.'

It's strange — it's more, it's frightening — how the mind works things out while keeping them unknown. What goes on in that territory? There's a moral failing somewhere. I had knowledge, pre-dated, at Joll's name, then leapt ahead, and sat for the rest of Mrs Maxey's story upright in my chair but collapsed inside, shifting, turning dazedly, in a nightmare of comprehension and helplessness. I found no place to be still.

The talk I've put down is approximate, and so will the rest of it be, when I put it down; but action and motive cut like knives.

Ferrabee boasted to 'Mary'. He came in primed for talk, and drank some more, and had her, I suppose (no, I don't suppose, I see it just as clearly as the rest), and told her how clever he had been. Look at the boss's car parked at the gate. He borrowed it whenever he liked. Look at this — a wad of fivers, his pay.

'I've got the old bugger where I want him,' he said.

He took her for a drive to Oriental Bay and pointed out the house where Owen Moody lived — the man Joll put a bullet through. He knew Moody pretty well, he said. (Ferrabee's a man who can go either way, Mrs Maxey explained.) As for Joll, he'd had his number right from the start, out at Akatarawa, at the camp. Ferrabee went into town next day, gave him a bit of cheek, got the job. But it didn't take him long to see where his chances lay. Joll called him to his club one day to pick him up after lunch. Ferrabee saw a man he recognised come out the door — a bloke he hadn't spotted for nine or ten years, when he was about sixteen. He'd got off the tram that night in Island Bay and walked past a car parked in the dark by the beach. The man inside gave a toot on his horn. He asked him if he'd like to go for a drive.

('That's impossible,' I said.

'Keep quiet, Sam. Just sit still,' Eric said.)

An easy five bob, Ferrabee said. He never saw the toffee-nose again until he stepped out of the Wellington Club and put on his hat and buttoned his coat and walked away. When Joll came out, Ferrabee described him: 'Poker up his bum,' he said (and Mrs Maxey apologised). Joll laughed. 'Poor old Jimmy Tinling. The man I'm going to beat for Parliament.'

Ferrabee boasts to his girl but hangs on to his secrets while they've still got work to do.

When he called at James's house the following day, he did not remind him of their meeting by the beach, and James made no sign of recognition. He sat in his chair; he watched and listened. It was like talking to a cobra snake, Ferrabee said.

'I thought so. I wondered,' James said, when Ferrabee told him Joll was a homosexual. Then he looked at Ferrabee a long time.

'And what do you want for yourself?'

'I'd rather work for you than him,' Ferrabee said.

I'm at it again, making up what people say. But I claim the right, and I claim rightness, and I'm not going to stop.

I don't know how long it took after that. How did the idea present itself — with a tickling in the mind, a furtive scuttle? And how long did it cling in the shadows on hooked legs before the place it found itself in became its rightful home? As far as I can tell, James accommodated it with no sense of invasion or defeat.

It was Ferrabee who said, 'Owen Moody'. It's possible that James thought of him first. I see him smile minutely when Ferrabee comes out with the name.

'Yes, he might serve.'

Ferrabee thinks 'serve' is a great joke.

James gives him a job as chauffeur and handyman. He allows him space in the garage for a bed. Later, after Violet's death, he lets him move into the house. There's a room off the kitchen. Ferrabee sleeps there. He torments Mrs Hearn into leaving. Then he's busy, busy, making himself useful, then indispensable. He's scarce when James wants him scarce and there when when he wants him there. He's out of sight, and in sight, one step ahead all the way.

'I can read that old bastard like a book. I know what he wants before he wants it,' Ferrabee says. ' "Ferrabee!" ' He mimics James's autocratic call. 'And I'm there. He doesn't know whether he's thought of something or it's me.'

Violet's death pushes Joll aside. Then, when it's time, Ferrabee plays the game of not mentioning him. It is James who says, 'You remember that chap Moody we were talking about . . . ?'

That was the hard part. Ferrabee wasn't sure of Owen Moody. He knew him from one or two encounters in places he went when he needed to earn ten bob. He ran into him and his boyfriend on the night of Eric's Donovan lecture — thought he might screw some cash out of them some time, except that Moody made him nervous. Ferrabee couldn't work out what part of his mind the bugger went to some of the time. 'Like,' he said to 'Mary', 'he'll go quiet, he'll go places you wouldn't want to be. He doesn't care except about number one.'

Ferrabee might have been describing himself.

'Do you know this man, Moody?' Mrs Maxey asked.

Eric told her we did.

'And his friend? The boy he lives with? Do you know him?' I saw that she knew of our relationship. 'As far as I can tell, from what Mary says, he didn't know anything about what was going on.'

I could only think of Freddie, and how having a son made his life supportable.

They recruited him. They picked him up in the car and drove to Lyall Bay, where James said, 'Go for a walk, Lennie. I'll call you when I need you.' Ferrabee walked on the beach. It did not bother him not to be in the know. Moody would do what he was hired for, and be gone. Ferrabee had James for longer than that: for as long as it took to milk him dry. Waves exploded, wetting him with spray. He turned his back to the southerly, made a cave of his chest, lit a cigarette — doing as he was told while pleasing himself. No hurry, he thought, I've got the rest of my life.

It took a lot of talking in the car; the two of them sitting in the dark, smoking James's Turkish cigarettes.

Moody is clear in my sight; he has no moral atmosphere, he's like the moon. James eludes me. Motive, yes, decision, yes, but where is self? Surely he destroys 'James Tinling'. There's a horrible wailing moment when nothing remains. If I can hear it, why can't he?

Moody leans forward and presses the horn. Ferrabee slouches back to his chauffeur seat. Asks no questions. He drives to Oriental Bay, where Moody gets out.

Events take their course after that. Ferrabee watches them unfold with glee. He planted the idea; the result belongs to him. It doesn't matter who works the details out, James or Moody. Every day that passes, every movement made, fixes him more firmly in place. Securing James satisfies him more than destroying Joll.

He meets Moody at the Post Office one Friday morning, gets Joll's letter and delivers it to James. There's another thing he knows.

Then Joll shoots Moody. Ferrabee goes down to the creek, where he can laugh. James had not wanted anyone hurt, or Joll's ruin so complete. He's afraid. Ferrabee works to calm him down. He 'tucks him up, feeds him porridge with a spoon'.

Ferrabee cements himself in.

'They'll offer it to you now. Wait and see.'

When she had finished, Mrs Maxey offered tea. I could not accept this return to normalcy. There was no leaving the place she had pushed us into. Six months have passed and I'm still there.

Eric questioned her but she had told all she knew. 'Mary', Ferrabee, James and Moody — her voice, her demeanour hold them frozen in a dance. That is an effect of memory. On the night of her telling they moved in lurid conjunctions and private frenzies. I'm a most susceptible man. I come too close and feel too hard and draw away before I understand. I turn side on, half bent, cover my face with my hands; use words too freely, before they set themselves. Use them in my head, and here on the page, but nothing gets to the point. I'm not unacquainted with 'the things of darkness' (Goethe) — have seen worse things than she told us, in my work, and squared them at the corners, made them firm in their joints. But when it touches me I lose my skills, I can't look straight.

What can I do? Simply describe.

She made tea and we drank it, in her cosy living room. We agreed not to do anything putting 'Mary' in danger. She saw us out and stood in the door as we drove away. I was filled with rancour against her. She would close her door, go back to her chair, pour herself another cup of tea, while out in the darkness Eric and I . . . what must we do?·

Nothing that night. We were held in a kind of stasis. Every step we might take turned into a half step. Rose and May, Freddie, Charlie blocked our way. And nothing would help Oliver Joll. He was in prison for shooting Moody. Entrapment was no excuse. He was past tense — yet has a huge presence, like the actor who fails to come on stage at his cue; and sometimes, when I consider those events, I see Ferrabee and Moody and James frozen in their gestures, waiting for him.

Eric drove to Oriental Bay and parked by the water. We looked across the harbour at the lights on Wadestown hill, at the distant lights of Petone, and now and then, sideways, at the house where Owen Moody and Taylor Barr lived. Shadows moved back and forth behind a yellow curtain. I wanted to bang on the door and shout at Taylor, unpick him, unknot him, make him safe, but Moody stopped me — like Ferrabee I was not sure where he would go to in his mind, and what violence he might perform.

'We need to think,' Eric said. His fingers made a hard insistent drumming on the wheel. My thoughts made a similar sort of drumming but could not move beyond the figures in Mrs Maxey's dance, where Eric and I stood on the margins, although joined. I could only declare, and repeat, We've got to get Taylor out of there.

'We can't do anything tonight,' Eric said. 'And listen, Sam. You'd better just let Taylor go.'

'What do you mean?'

'You can't change him. He's that way. Let's think about what we do with Moody and James.'

We argued and I shouted and he hammered on the wheel. It was midnight when he dropped me at my gate. I went to bed, where Rose was sleeping. She had been helping May all afternoon with her work for the Women's Welfare League — was going up there daily, which I could not prevent. It tired her and refreshed her and turned her, in some concerns, side on to me.

Now I stood side on to her.

I had said to Eric, at the end, 'We'll put them in prison.'

He turned away from me. 'How, Sam? There's no evidence. And don't you think James is there already?'

Twelve

wen Moody opened the door. Perhaps his intuition was sharpened by fear, but after his initial shock, in which he knew our purpose, he smiled and made a mocking half-bow: 'Gentlemen. Step inside.' He was wearing slippers, a silk dressing-gown, a cravat — his get-up for writing, I suppose. A typewriter stood on a desk looking over the bay, with an inch-thick pile of paper beside it and a sheet, half written, curling out.

'My novel,' he said, seeing my glance. 'I have to thank you for getting me started, Sam. I might have wasted years on poetry.'

'What is it?' Eric said. 'A murder story?'

'Detective. I don't mind telling you, I'm good at it. It's as easy as my mother knitting socks. The stuff pours out. I've already thought of half a dozen more I can write.'

'I suppose you think you're going to be rich and famous?' I said.

'Yes, I will be. You're not going to be jealous, Sam? Getting shot gives me inside running, in a way.'

'And telling lies in court,' I said.

'I was never there. I was in hospital, remember.'

'Your statement —'

'Sam,' Eric said. We had agreed in the car that he would do the talking.

'Sit down, why don't you?' Moody said, and when we would not, said, 'Well, I'm going to be comfortable.' He took his seat in one of the two easy chairs in the room. Then he crossed his legs, folded his arms, smiled at us in his down-looking way, although looking up. 'I'll tell you now, there's nothing you can say I want to hear.'

Eric seemed to relax. It was as if he'd understood the rules of a game. He sat in the other chair and smiled back at Moody. 'You're quite a fellow.'

'I know where I'm going. It's a long way from here.'

'You're going to prison. Where you've put Joll,' I said.

He gave me a glance, then ignored me. 'What do you think you know, Professor?'

Watching them, I thought there was no end to the ways each could turn. Eric's largeness gave him space, while Moody would invent endlessly, step anywhere, to increase and please himself. I saw, beyond my distaste, that he was a fellow who would impress — a good-looking confident man. I could not see the sexual invert in him, but only masculine ways and looks. There was a little preening, that was all: a smoothing of his hair, a tidying of his dressing gown.

'So?' he said, inviting Eric.

'We're really not much concerned with you, Owen. We just thought you might put us straight on one or two things. Like, Ollie Joll's endorsement on your statement. There's some curious wording there, don't you think?'

'How, curious? He admits it's true.'

'Substantially true, he says. And only so far as it relates "to his own act and deed". What about yours, Owen? Your act and deed?'

'I wrote down exactly what I did.'

'Did you write down why? I know you were only James Tinling's tool, but you'd know a fair bit.'

Moody's mouth gave an ugly twist at 'tool'. He reached for his cigarettes and lit one. 'I could throw you out of here. But I'm curious to know what you think you're playing at. Has trying to write detective stories made you believe you're Sherlock Holmes?' He grinned at me. 'And Doctor Watson?'

'There's a man in prison,' I began.

'For shooting me. The bullet went in here.' He tapped his chest. 'Do you want to see the scar? It nicked my lung. Anyone else would be dead.'

'Joll's as good as dead. You trapped him into it.'

His brief attention to me turned into contempt. He drew in smoke, then let it out with jutted underlip: 'Ah, no.' He cancelled me and smiled at Eric. 'It happened exactly how I said in my statement. I wish I could write it properly. I was pretty sick. I had to dictate. There's stuff I left out. Like, how Joll couldn't stop touching me, getting my wrist —' demonstrating — 'and squeezing my shoulder. Filthy devil, trying me out.' He smiled. 'But I didn't want to say all that because of his poor wife.'

'Aren't you a homosexual yourself?' Eric said.

'Good heavens, no. I just enjoy male company. I'm enjoying myself now.'

'It's your own business, of course. But it seems hypocritical pretending Ollie Joll disgusted you. That's what bothers me, not what you are.'

'What I am?'

'You can fill in the name. I'm curious that money means more to you, that's all.'

'Do you think we're a club? We're all blood brothers?' Moody said. His sudden fury startled me.

'I think you'd betray anyone,' Eric replied. 'But I would have supposed some fellow feeling with Joll. Both of you having to pretend.'

Moody stared. He might explode. Then he mashed out his cigarette. 'Ha. Very clever. You can't get me one way, so you'll try another. Playing on my sympathy for Joll. Well I've got none. He was a toad. I've put him exactly where he belongs.'

'Tell me about James Tinling then,' Eric said.

'I have fellow feeling with him.'

'If you mean he's a homosexual too, we know that. I'm more interested in your money arrangements.'

'I have no money arrangements with Mr Tinling. I've met him once or twice. He's a friendly man. We agree about politics. ' Moody began to enjoy himself. 'As for him being a homosexual, as you call it, isn't that slanderous? I think he could take you to court. He would, if I told him, brothers-in-law or not.'

'He wanted to get Joll out of the way, didn't he? So he hired you to compromise him — knowing from his little man, Ferrabee, that you know how to set up things like that. It's a nasty story, Owen, and your part is one of the worst, but let's agree that getting shot pays you back. We're not after you, we're gunning for James. I think you've confirmed all we need to know.'

'Dogshit, Professor. I've said nothing.' Moody smiled with false ease. He was wound up. He wanted to be himself. 'But you know, as a writer, the only one here —' he flashed a smile of contempt at me: more than contempt, 'salt scorn', the poet says — 'I'm interested in this story you're making up. It seems like a good one. So please carry on.'

'James got in touch with you through Ferrabee. You worked out a plan to trap Joll — get him to make sexual overtures to you, so you could play the virtuous young citizen and expose him. Or threaten to. Get him out of the way so James could stand in the Melling seat. Your part is banal, although I've no doubt you enjoyed yourself, pulling down a better man than you. That's

194

what attracted you. And the money, of course.'

'Listen,' Moody cried, but Eric went on: 'You're a dull chappie, Owen. Both sorts of greed are in plentiful supply. James Tinling is the dangerous one. He just pointed you like a gun.'

'You think so? I can wreck him if I want to, as easy as Joll. I can bust him in pieces —' he snapped his fingers — 'like that. You think you're going to punish me somehow. But if you make a single move against me I'll bring him down. If you think Joll made a loud noise, wait till you hear that one. I've got stuff written down. I've done the whole story and put it where it's safe, so he can't send Ferrabee round.'

'So you're blackmailing James?'

'I could blackmail him for more than Joll. But I won't be greedy. I won't need the Honourable James Tinling soon. Just enough to get me started over there. And why not? You think I haven't done my share of chipping weeds and slashing gorse? I've worn the skin off my hands stacking bricks, ever done that? And adding up stuff in a ledger — how much money someone else is raking in, the crooks. For four pounds two and six a week. I've finished with it.'

'How much for perjuring yourself?' I said.

'Ah, you're shocked, little Sam. Are you shocked, Professor? There's ways of looking at life you've never dreamed of. Perfectly good ones too. So play your little games. Morality and justice, isn't it? How dull.'

'We'll put all three of you in prison,' I said.

'No you won't. You won't get Joll out either. There's no proof anywhere. It's all in your head.'

Eric smiled and stood up. 'Yes, quite right. We just thought we'd have a look at you.'

'Was it worth it?'

'Oh yes.'

'What do you see?'

'Nothing much. Don't go after compliments, Owen. There's dozens of clever little tykes like you. Are you ready, Sam?'

'There's one more thing.' I faced Moody, who lounged in his chair, riding Eric's insult, keeping it down. 'You can go away, and stay away, and good riddance too, but you're not taking Taylor Barr with you.'

'Who says I'm not?' Moody smiled as if I'd offered the compliment Eric denied. 'It'll break his heart. He's set on it.'

'You can get on your ship. We'll let you do that —'

'You will?'

'We know what you've turned him into, Moody.'

'Oh dear, oh dear.'

'But you're not going to corrupt him any more. You go, he stays. If not, I'll tell him all about you and Joll.'

'Ah.' Moody took his time. He lit another cigarette. 'What you're overlooking, Sam, is that he knows already.' He grinned at me. 'And it thrills him. He thinks I'm evil. Taylor's got a very naughty streak. And Sam —' how the fellow acted, picking a tobacco thread off his tongue — 'if you do the slightest thing to upset him, I'll pay a little visit on his Ma and Pa. I think they're still in blissful ignorance, aren't they?'

'If you do that . . .' I had nothing to threaten him with.

He waited, smiled, said, 'What?'

'He's too young. He should stay here.'

'But it's like Noel Coward says, "I'm wild about the boy." '

'Come on, Sam,' Eric said. He led me to the door.

'Oh, Professor, if you don't mind some advice,' Moody said. 'Lifebuoy soap for that BO.'

'Ha!' Eric said.

'No, you're supposed to say, "Thanks, Owen, you're a brick." '

196

Eric dismissed him by turning away. But out in the street he said, almost complacently, 'I've always been a heavy sweater.'

We drove along the road by the harbour and north through Petone to Lower Hutt. Charlie was in town for her lesson with Frank Siers — although, as Eric said, it would make more sense for her to be teaching him.

The trees on James's front lawn were weighted with leaves, yet had the upward springing of the season. The flower beds shimmered with bees.

'What do we do if Ferrabee's home?'

'Ignore him. James won't let him in while we're talking.'

I was not so sure. Ferrabee's self-conceit was shallower than Moody's and more likely to spring out. He might force his way into the room; would bite and tear if he felt himself in danger.

We drew up by the garage. It was empty. Eric walked back and tried the front door. He peered through the letter slot, then rang the bell, a tinkling thing screwed to the wall. It made me think of Violet's handbell by her bed. Now that she was dead, the house seemed hers as much as James's.

We went around to the back of the house and found him dozing on the chaise longue. A handkerchief folded lengthwise covered his eyes. Eric plucked it off and dropped it on his chest.

'Wake up, James.'

His eyelids opened with a snap but he remained unseeing for a moment, with an old man's bewilderment. I had never seen James so naked. It made me ashamed, and I said, 'It's Sam and Eric. We want to talk to you, James.'

'Sam. Eric. Good heavens.' He sat up. The movement made him dizzy. 'I must — what is it? Is something wrong?'

'We'll only keep you a minute,' Eric said.

'This is — I take exception. Ferrabee!' he called.

'He's gone to his girl. There's only us.'

'Yes. All right. Tweedledum and Tweedledee. What is it you want?' He made a bony thrusting of his lower face, a movement used to put himself in charge. Eric grinned.

'Sit and listen, James. And get that lawyer's look off your face, we've seen it too much. We're going to tell you a story about Owen Moody and Oliver Joll.'

I did not like Eric's tone. I wanted something judicious — judicial too — and James reduced by more than bullying.

He made a shiver at the names, then contracted in some way, armed himself with his practised cold authority. 'I don't have time for claptrap. And I won't be trespassed on.'

He began to stand, but Eric put his hand on his shoulder and held him down.

'Sit still, James. We won't be long. There's just a few things we want you to understand. Then you can go back to sleep.'

'Eric,' I began.

'Keep quiet, Sam.' I did not understand his animosity. It seemed more intimate, determinate, than moral.

'This is an assault. Putting your hand on me is assault,' James said.

'That's right. You can have me arrested. But I'll have quite a story to tell.'

'Take your hand away.'

Eric released him. He pulled a wicker chair close and sat down facing James. 'You don't like touching, do you? Only boys.'

'What? What do you say?'

'Boys, James. Well, maybe young men. I don't suppose Ferrabee's too old.'

James made a panting noise, trying to speak. His cheeks, flushed from sleeping, turned a waxy yellow-white.

'You've had a long time behind your mask,' Eric said.

'How dare . . .' James managed to get out.

Eric patted him. 'Rest easy, old boy. Sam and I are the only ones who know. And we're going to leave you in there all by yourself.'

'I don't know what you're talking about.'

'You know very well. You're an amazing fellow, James. Living your public life as an act of will. And making it work. I take my hat off to you. What's it been like in the little room out the back?'

'Will you leave now? Will you leave?'

'In a minute. There's just this business with Moody and Joll. Did you really have to do that to Ollie?'

'I don't know Moody. I scarcely knew Joll.'

'Fifteen years' hard labour he's doing, James.'

'He shot a man.'

'What about the things that came before? You and Moody and Ferrabee setting it up? Coaxing Joll in like a pheasant into a cage. Have you still got his letter?'

'I know nothing about letters. I'm calling the police.'

'Don't do that. If Ferrabee gets sight of a cop, he'll squeal. I'll bet on it. So will Moody, when the chips are down. Have you thought about jail, James? You'll have a cell alongside Ollie Joll. They won't make you crack rocks though. Old men sew mail bags.'

'The pair of you disgust me,' James said.

'James,' I began, wanting to reason with him, make him *see*, but he sent his usual flick of denial at me.

'I haven't spent my life scribbling lies in newspapers. Or —' suddenly at Eric — 'staring at the moon through a telescope. I'm a respected lawyer: ask my fellow lawyers what I am. I've lived a good life. And you two ... With a man like Joll. He had language like a navvy. He was a pervert.'

'Don't you do the same sort of thing?' Eric said.

'I do not. I do not. I've lived out here forty years. I've lived like a monk.'

'But you go over the wall, don't you James, when you feel the urge?'

James raised his voice and cried, 'Ferrabee!'

'I told you, he's gone to his girl,' Eric said.

'Leave him,' I said. I did not know why I felt pity for James, yet there it was, making me say, 'Just tell him what we came for. Then let's go.'

'If you spread this story about,' James said.

'We won't. We're just letting you know we know, that's all. You and Moody working out how to get Joll to make his move. I'll bet Moody gave him some come-ons, eh? Then telling him he'd have to resign. It's a neat trick, James. But Moody getting shot wasn't part of the plan. It must have given you a nasty turn. Well, now we're leaving you to get on with your own hard labour. Fifteen years. Do you think you'll last?'

Eric stood up.

'You can't run for Parliament. You'll have to resign,' I said.

He heard me for perhaps the first time in his life, and rose from the chaise longue to his full height. It was as if his stance would tell him what to say, but his mouth only opened and closed and nothing came out. His face took on a puzzled look. Then he drew himself in, and down, and was suddenly intimate. 'Do you understand,' he whispered, 'what my life's been like? Living with that woman and making my career in spite of her?'

'Whatever it's been like for you, it was worse for Violet. Come on, Sam.'

'Every day I spent, she was like a slug crawling on my face, do you understand? I couldn't get rid of her; she was always there. Sam, you knew her, you saw how she tried to ruin me. I would have been, if it wasn't for her, you know what I would have been. Prime Minister. But she held me down. She crawled on me, I couldn't get her off. Well, now she's gone. And Joll is gone. I can be . . .' He put his hand on my arm, making me recoil. 'You mustn't stand in my way.'

'We're not going to,' Eric said. 'Come on, Sam.'

'But we can't let him —'

'Yes, we can.' He pulled my arm. 'I want to get out of here.' He led me to the corner of the house.

I freed myself and looked back. James stood beyond the forest of roses — a stick of a man, dry and dead. All those years of deferring to him, of recoiling from the small hard stumps of feeling he exposed — rudimentary? vestigial? I could never tell — and being drawn back by his certainties; the weight of his life, all the gravity and fineness. What were they now? A page of newsprint crumpled up and thrown into a corner.

I turned away, not wanting him marked on me in any way, and followed Eric to the car.

'I thought we were stopping him,' I said.

'He thinks he's going to win the Melling seat. But Drake will beat him. Getting rid of Joll is all for nothing. What do you think James is left with then?'

We had no time to take it further, for Ferrabee's car came through the gate and blocked our way. He jumped out and ran to Eric's window.

'What do you two want?'

'Ask your boss,' Eric said.

'You've done something to him.' He ran back to his car and turned off the ignition. 'You're not getting away from here.' He went to the front door and let himself in. 'Mr Tinling,' he cried.

'Now's my chance to let his tyres down,' Eric said.

'No —'

'Joking, Sam. It's time for a bit of cross-country driving.' He eased the car over the flowering border, drove it in a half circle on the lawn, scraping its roof on ngaio branches, crossed the border again behind Ferrabee's car, gave a toot on his horn, and went out the gate.

'Shouldn't we get Charlie away from there?'

'She wants to stay till after the election. Then she's shifting into town.' He drove through Petone. 'Smile, Sam.'

'It doesn't seem enough.'

'It is for James. Leave him alone, he'll fall off the wall. I don't know about the other two.'

So we left them on that day, having done all we could. Eric dropped me at my gate. I sat in the summer house with a glass of beer, considering our imperfect closure, our wrapping up of those things I've written about, less than one week before the election.

Thirteen

Taylor and Owen Moody sailed away on Tuesday 26 November. I was walking, solitary, in Barnard Street, when I saw the *Ionic* turn awkwardly from the wharf, then take on dignity as it steamed towards Point Jerningham. Soon the hills on either side sucked it in and only the wake remained, a silver scar. The dangerous one and his catamite were gone; they were erased, although for Freddie and Elsie there would be a bending to the north, to the child they imagined there. They would call his name but Taylor would not answer. Silence from London, but an inner crying in Wellington — until, perhaps, one day he crept home. Freddie would open his arms, in whatever state Taylor arrived.

The next morning Rose and I walked out to vote. There was a sabbatical calm in the streets, a hush and echo in our polling booth. The change we expected (I broke the habit of a lifetime, voting Labour) slept like some indifferent beast. I felt like stamping my shoe on the pavement: Wake up, wake up.

We spent the afternoon in our garden, weeding side by side with trowel and fork. Late in the afternoon I mowed the lawns, and the chatter of the blades put some urgency at last into election day. I felt a breaking out of excitement and a need, which I contained, to call over the fence to my neighbour: Any news?

By seven o'clock people were streaming past our gate. We waited until eight for Eric and May, hurried out when his car arrived, and walked in a quartet round to Lambton Quay, where the crowd was like a rugby test-match crowd flowing up the street, except that there were more women than a match would draw.

We side-stepped into Featherston Street, then to Victoria, but could find no better place than the back of the crowd. Ahead of us a field of hats, gleaming like clods of earth, stretched across the concourse of streets to the *Dominion* building, where the results board masked the first and second storeys. There were thirty thousand people gathered in the windless air, exhaling, breathing easily, only half awake, knowing change but not its onrushing yet, and its overturning of the squat governance we were used to.

We were too far back to read the board, but loudspeakers called progress reports. A moment came, only a quarter of an hour after we arrived, when it was known, not from posted or called results, but by a ripple of prescience in the crowd, followed by a vertiginous tipping. There was a lurch of sound, a bawl, a baying: Labour had won. It rolled like curled earth from a plough, turning the old parties out. After that upheaval and long shout only a happy murmuring remained, broken now and then by cheers as each new result boomed out. We heard Wellington as though it were the whole country: Wellington Central, then South and East and North (our electorate), Labour all. Only Wellington Suburbs stayed with the Nationalists.

'Melling?' May said. 'What's happened to James?'

'He's gone,' Eric said, sharp eyed. 'Drake has squashed him flat.'

'Listen, listen,' I said.

'Drake, Labour, six thousand eight hundred and forty-three,' the loud speaker boomed. 'Gleeson, Douglas Credit, four hundred and twenty-nine. Small, Democrat, two hundred and thirty-four. Tinling, Nationalist, three thousand and one.'

'And one, and one,' echoed off the buildings behind us.

'Goodnight, James Tinling,' Eric said.

'Oh, don't be cruel,' Rose said. Her eyes filled with tears. She found her handkerchief and pressed them dry.

'Where will he be? They're going to do speeches,' May said.

'In Melling. It's only the locals here.'

'James will be home with his front door locked,' I said. I felt no gloating, but a sadness in my heart, the same feeling that had brought tears to Rose's eyes. I clutched her hand, but said in a hardy tone: 'Bolted tight.'

We stayed for the speeches, which were modest, jocular, shallow, insincere — 'Why don't they crow, they should rub it in,' May said — from the winners, and oozing with good sportsmanship and democratic platitudes from the rest.

It was close to midnight when we walked home. Remembering that quake or tremor in the crowd, I joked that the pavement should be split, the faces of buildings fallen off and everything twisted round to face the other way.

'It's more like a tidal wave. Everything washed clean,' Rose said.

'There are dead fish after tidal waves, my dear. These fellows are politicians after all,' Eric said.

'But good ones,' May cried. 'They care.'

'That would take a shaft of light from heaven.'

'There was one, did you see?'

He caught her by the waist and swung her round, both of them laughing.

But underneath our buoyancy lay James Tinling. His corpse, although political, belonged to his family. Rose wondered what he would do, where he would go.

'He'll have Charlie with him,' she said.

Eric and I kept quiet. It was more likely James would have Ferrabee.

'She's shifting into town. Not before time,' May said. 'James will turn her into an old maid out there.'

I let the others worry about her — she was simple. But I could not see James. Owen Moody, I could: fascinating, horrifying in his purity — pure self-absorption. Was James harder to find only because I'd known him for so long?

I pictured him in his chair in his darkened room, turning over his unlived life — his monkish life — and his crime, while somewhere in the shadows Ferrabee lurked. Their world was changed by the tremor too. Like my twisted buildings, they faced another way.

I could imagine nothing he might do but keep on sitting. His room was like the prison he had put Ollie Joll in.

Fourteen

*I*t is late autumn, a time of slow breezes and soft rain. Leaves lie raked in corners, where I've left them to rot. We'll have our winter storms before long. It is five months since I began telling our story — Eric's and James's and Charlie's and mine. There's still a bit of it left to write, but I'm afflicted with fear and unwillingness — and why those two? Shouldn't I look forward to being free and so hurry on to my conclusion? I see the time when I'll stand up from my desk and stretch my arms above my head and hear the vertebrae go click in my back, but I don't see peace and freedom as I turn to leave; I don't feel the warmth of completion or a settling in the molecules of remembered act and decision.

People carry on with their lives. Why should it surprise me? Did I suppose they would stop their progress and be still just because I fixed them in tableaux?

This morning there's an item in the *Dominion*: 'A young New Zealander, Owen Moody, has scored a critical success in London with the publication of his first novel, a detective story called *Blood in the basement*. Favourable reviews have appeared in several London daily newspapers and the young author is already hard at work on his second novel. Wellingtonians will remember Mr Moody as the unfortunate victim in a shooting...'

I daresay we'll see it in our bookshops before long. I won't buy it.

I won't read it. Won't help him even with ten per cent of seven and sixpence.

I see Moody in smoking jacket and silk cravat, with brilliantined hair (even though his hair was never like that), sitting at a typewriter in his London flat. He smokes a Turkish cigarette. There's a smiling scar on his mouth. Now that he is moving again, everything mixes up.

Has he got rid of Taylor Barr? London must be full of young men.

I won't read his novel but have just re-read his chapter. I've tied it in its pink tape with the others and hope I'll never see it again. I'll say what I know: Owen Moody writes well. I'm stupid to have held the belief that good writing, of whatever sort, rests on virtue.

James was the one who smoked Turkish cigarettes. Moody's writing rests on cleverness. I've thought of being clever myself and writing the end of my book as an action story: the Professor drives to the rescue; confronts the villain and his henchman; saves the maiden; a secret is revealed — but I can't. I've come this far with open eyes and mustn't put on blinkers now, even though they'd help me present the facts without the messy outrage I go in for. Eric told me once that I had a sniffy nose. He meant my moralist's nose; and he went on to argue that my sort of seriousness is replaced in modern times by inclusiveness — human inclusiveness, he called it (implying that my judging is inhuman). If that is so — and the evidence suggests he's right — the history of behaviour turns a corner (just as, in the year I've written about, politics turned). But morality is human, isn't it? It is where we've got to and is fixed now in our blood. The sort of looseness Eric makes himself a spokesman for doesn't lead forward but back down the road. On one side path it leads us to Ferrabee and Moody and James.

At mid-morning on the day after election day, May telephoned: 'Sam, can you go out and intercept Eric. He's walking over to the observatory. He should be just about on Tinakori Road.'

'What for?' I asked.

'Charlie phoned. She's in a state. James is on some sort of rampage. She wants Eric to go there. Can you hurry?'

I put on my jacket, called to Rose that I wouldn't be long, and walked round to the top of Molesworth Street, where I found Eric crossing. We hurried back up the hill and he unlocked his garage. May called from the window, 'She's on the phone again. I can't tell what's wrong. Can you talk to her?'

'Charlie,' I said, 'what's going on?'

'He's smashing everything Mother owned. He's even tearing curtains down. Can Eric come? I'm trying to pack. I've got to leave.'

Eric hurried in and snatched the phone, but when he spoke Ferrabee answered. Eric cried, 'You put my niece back on, Ferrabee. If you touch her —'

The phone went dead.

'What did he say?'

'She's not well, she needs to lie down. That bastard . . .' He ran to the car.

'Go with him, Sam,' May cried.

We drove along the harbour road at speeds of sixty and seventy miles an hour.

'He took the phone off her. I heard her scream.'

'We should have telephoned the police.'

213

'We'll get there before any police,' Eric said.

It took twenty minutes. I thought we would find Charlie dead. The entrance gates on the drive were padlocked. Eric pressed the car on them until the bolt sprang free. We drove to the front door, where I held his arm: 'Eric, be careful.' He seemed misproportioned by his fear and rage, and I felt we might meet beings in the house unshaped in some similar way — James and Ferrabee unnatural, homicidal. He rattled the door, then ran round to the back of the house. We saw Ferrabee busy at a fire by the creek, throwing flattened boxes on the flames.

Eric ran inside as though bursting through scrub. We went past the kitchen into the hall and found tipped furniture, torn hangings, a broken mirror. He turned in a circle, lost, then swelled his throat and bellowed, 'Charlie!'

She cried from upstairs, behind her door, 'They've locked me in.'

He ran up, three steps at a time, faced the door, heaved on it with his shoulder, then stood back. I've seen it done in movies — a horizontal stamp, human horse-kick, at the lock. The door bursts in. Not for Eric, and I thought, He'll kill himself, he's too old. I found a key on the hall stand.

'Eric, here.'

He turned it in the lock, rushed in, as James leaned from his study door.

'You're a fool, James. You can't lock up a grown woman,' I cried.

He stepped to the hall door and screamed, 'Ferrabee.'

'James, think what you're doing.' I ran down the stairs and took his shoulders, looked in his face, which was raw on one cheekbone where he had injured himself tearing things down. He beat me with his hands, birdwing hands, forcing me back.

'Ferrabee, stop them,' he said.

He appears like a manifestation, Ferrabee; he's suddenly there.

Although I'm not a man of action I hooked my foot on his shin. Saw his falling as a vision of rightness. Then he was upright and prancing on the stairs. Charlie and Eric stood at the top, with a suitcase each.

'Get back,' Eric cried, swinging his case.

Ferrabee tumbled again. He stopped himself with a grabbing hand on the rail, lay printed there, with bloody mouth. He spat a broken tooth out, moved again, would not be stopped; but Charlie screamed, 'I'll tell the police what you did. He was touching me —' to James and Eric — 'when he locked me in. He was putting his hands here and here.' She pressed her hand on her breasts and between her thighs. 'It was on purpose. You'll go to prison.'

It stopped Ferrabee as blows could not. He might think himself in a world where inclination ruled — lust and greed — protected by James Tinling's fiat, but he understood 'prison' all right and did not mean to end up there.

'We're going now,' Charlie said, imperious. 'Da, we're going. I won't stay here any more.'

'Go then. Get out of my house,' James said.

Charlie and Eric came down the stairs, shunting Ferrabee. I saw how he longed to attack.

'Come here, Ferrabee,' James said, as though calling a dog.

'Sam, Eric,' Charlie said, when she reached the foot, 'will you put my paintings in the car. I won't take a single thing else,' she said to James.

Ferrabee grinned through his blood. 'Too late.'

'They were filth,' James said. 'I had every right.'

I made sense of the flat objects and the fire. 'He was burning them.'

'I won't have filth in my house,' James said.

Charlie ran past me, and Ferrabee called, 'You can toast some sausages. Do one for me.'

'Go with her, Sam,' Eric said.

I did not know where I should be. Eric and Ferrabee were not finished yet. I went to the back door and saw Charlie running. The fire burned in its centre and smoked at the edge. She stood helplessly, half ran to the stream, ran back and plucked a painting from the flames. It flickered as she ran holding it away from her. She plunged it in the stream. I imagined the hiss, and her sob. She looked at it, laid it down, then sat and put her head in her arms.

I turned back to the hall and saw Ferrabee spread his hands. I heard him say, 'I surrender all my rights, Prof. You can give her one. She's dying for it.'

Perhaps he thought Eric would grapple with him, or set himself for a boxer's punch. He was not ready for a clubbing back-handed blow. It took him on the mouth. The smack sickened me, yet his reeling to the wall, the little man, Ferrabee, and sliding down, filled me with elation. Then it was gone. I ran to Eric, grabbed at him two-handed, tried to drag him out of the house. 'Have you gone mad?'

He shook me off and faced James, who was bent in the middle, like a cracked clothes prop, and gasping for air.

'Don't hit him,' I cried, coming back at Eric. He held my shirt-front, easy now, and said to James, 'That was for you. He's your proxy.'

James did not hear. He made a little cry of love and sat by Ferrabee at the wall. He took him in his arms — the man gagging and spitting — then freed one arm and felt in his pocket.

'Sam,' he said, piteous, 'a handkerchief.'

I gave him mine. He wiped Ferrabee's mouth. 'Lennie, dear boy, it's all right, you'll be all right.' Then to us, pleading and courteous: 'Will you go away now.'

We went out to Charlie by the stream. She was lying on her back, but turned on her elbow when she heard us, giving a smile I could not guess the meaning of. The painting she had saved lay face down on the grass. She stood it up for us to see.

'It's the only one left.'

The fire had scorched the frame along the bottom, burned a hole where James's feet had been, and made the canvas bubble across his face. It charred Violet down the length of her body, but left her face china white and pure, as if some other dispensation held.

'Do you want to keep it, Eric? I promised it to you.'

'No,' he said. He took it and walked to the fire; held it upright with a hooked finger; let it fall face down; watched it burn.

'I'm glad to have all that old stuff gone,' Charlie said. Yet she was grieving, and grieving for her father in the house.

'Is there anything you need from in there?' Eric said.

'No, nothing.'

'Do you you want your paints and canvases?'

'Yes, I suppose so.'

We carried them from the shed — canvases, paints, brushes, easel, books — and put them with her suitcases in the car, watching all the time for movements in the house.

Eric winced with pain. 'Sam, will you drive? I think I've broken something in my hand.'

'I won't even look back,' Charlie said, falsely brave.

Halfway to Wellington she began to weep, but dried her eyes and composed herself as we turned up the hill to Eric's house.

May had telephoned Rose. They took Charlie to the sitting room. I carried her belongings in while Eric bathed his hand. I found him in the bathroom, trying to bandage it.

'I'll get May.'

'No, leave her. Tie these ends for me.' His face was white with pain. 'I haven't punched anyone since I boxed at school.'

'You need an X-ray,' I said.

217

'Later. Let's see how they are.'

We came into the sitting room in time to hear Charlie say, 'I'm going to marry Frank Siers.'

'No you're not,' Eric said.

'Eric,' May warned.

'He's twenty years older than you. And he's a fool.'

Charlie flushed. Her tears began again, instantly. 'He's a kind man. And he won't bother me. I'll have a place to paint.'

'I won't let you.'

'Eric, be quiet,' May said.

'She can't marry someone like that.'

May stood up. She faced him, leaning forward as though to bite. 'Go outside. Go away. And don't come back in here until I say.'

'May —'

'Now, Eric.' There's a kind of boiling coldness she generates. Eric can do nothing against it. He blundered out.

'You too, Sam.'

I followed him across the lawn and down into the garden, where we sat on a bench facing the harbour. He nursed his hand. After a while, I said, 'She really is your daughter, isn't she?'

'Yes,' he said.

'How did it happen?'

'It isn't the sort of thing you want to know, Sam.'

'Probably not. Does May know?'

'Of course she does.'

'And Rose?'

'They're sisters. They talk.'

'So I'm the only one who doesn't?'

'You. And Charlie. And James.'

'He doesn't?'

'He doesn't know who. I don't —' Eric tried to smile — 'come within his frame of acceptability.'

'Will May tell Charlie now?'

'I hope not. But you never know with her.'

'Charlie only needs to look at you, then in the mirror.' I was astonished that I hadn't seen it before.

He reached with his good hand for his tobacco. I took it from him and rolled two cigarettes. We smoked side by side, although I would have preferred my pipe.

He said, 'She was a sad woman. But perfectly normal in most ways. She could have got the marriage annulled. Or got a boy-friend. James would have looked the other way.' He smoked a while, then grinned maliciously. 'You would have been acceptable. More the gentleman.'

'Was it before you married May? It must have been.'

'I knew that's what you'd ask. Yes, it was. Though we were engaged. To everyone's consternation, eh Sam? Violet's especially. I wonder how it was that an oaf like me was the only one who could see what was wrong with her.'

'Did it go on long?'

'I could ask your questions for you. It's odd how you and I stay friends.'

'I suppose you're going to say you did it for her?'

'No, Sam, that's what you'd say. I did it for me. But I felt pretty sure she'd enjoy it too.'

He had touched her by accident one day, walking in the garden — and heard her gasp and felt her tremble. He rode his bicycle out to Lower Hutt the next morning, when he knew James would be at work.

'I had to go easy, Sam. Not frighten her. But once she'd got the hang of it we kept going all day. I was just the sort of stud bull she needed. So once in her life . . .' He grinned. 'No, that's lies. Like I said, I did it for me. But when I tried going back next day she'd turned into the Violet we all knew. Couldn't go on with it. She was terrified.'

'What of?'

'Losing her nice house, I suppose. And not being Mrs Tinling any more. And maybe Lady Tinling at some future date.' Eric laughed. 'We all know how hungry she was for that. But as well . . .'

I waited.

'Getting pregnant. And maybe just enjoying herself. Because she really did, with bells on, Sam. She was pretty sore down there, I could tell by the way she walked.'

'For God's sake, Eric.'

'You want the truth, don't you? Maybe she thought sore was punishment for liking it. So she said she'd say I'd raped her if I didn't get out. I told her she should bolt. Head for another town. Get another man. Then I rode my bike back home.'

'Are you saying you'd have married her if she'd left James?'

'God, no. Married? With Vi? When I had May? But it was amazing, Sam. You don't get that sort of thing, that surprise and greed . . . Now you look as if you'll slit my throat. May knows about it. She was glad about Charlie when she knew she couldn't have children herself.'

'And James and Violet carried on pretending.'

'She should have left. I'd have helped with that.'

'The way Charlie's going to be pretending with Frank Siers.'

He threw his cigarette butt down the garden, then looked over his shoulder at the house. May was at the sitting room window, watching us. He turned away, put his hands on his knees, winced with pain. He said, after another while: 'Frank Siers, eh? He'd better not spoil Charlie's painting, that's all I say.'

I drove him to the hospital for an X-ray. A bone was broken in his hand. He looked pleased with himself, and was pleased with his arm in a sling when, some hours later, I delivered him to May.

Rose and I walked down the hill. A squall of rain arrived as we reached our gate. We ran inside and locked the door.

Now I can put an end to it — an end of sorts. I'm looking for a good man in my story, but can find only Freddie Barr, whom I once despised. There's one good woman I am sure of: Rose, my wife. About the rest, I'm not competent to say. Not really competent for judging at all.

Oliver Joll labours through his first year in prison. Moody and Taylor Barr stay in London, together or alone I do not know. James lives in his Lower Hutt house with his man Ferrabee. I've nothing more to say about them.

May works on as secretary of her women's group but Rose is growing tired and helps her less. Charlie has become Mrs Siers. She paints busily in his — in their — studio. I don't like what she's doing now any more than I liked the paintings James had Ferrabee burn — or the one in Rose's sewing room. Eric reserves his decision.

I'm getting to the end, wrapping up. Eric is left. What is there to say about him?

Last night I walked up Glenmore Street to visit Roy Kember. He has fallen even deeper into depression, and perhaps senility, it's hard to tell. I sat with him for half an hour but he recognised me only in starts, and spoke my name without liking or dislike, without any feeling at all.

I left him and walked down to Tinakori Road. I was passing the Western Park Hotel when I saw Eric's car pull up outside Mrs

Maxey's house. He got out, unsecretive, and knocked his rat-tat, rat-tat-tat on her door. After she had let him in I crossed the road and looked to see if they went upstairs. No light went on up there. Instead I heard the piano playing. Eric sang, distantly, in his baritone: 'I did but see her passing by, And yet I love her till I die . . .'

I don't know what is going on; or what goes on anywhere.

The moon came up — Shelley's 'crystal paramour', Milton's 'spotty globe'. There are thousands of descriptions to pick from. It joined with the streetlights, swallowing the stars. I could not see Eric's doubles and variables.

I'll close my notebook and lock it with its fellows in my bottom drawer.

Nothing ends except my telling.

LIMERICK COUNTY LIBRARY

ACKNOWLEDGEMENTS AND NOTE

The staff of the Manuscripts and Archives Section of the Alexander Turnbull Library found a number of useful items for me, including accounts of the trial (in 1920) of C. E. Mackay, Mayor of Wanganui, for the attempted murder of the poet D'Arcy Cresswell, and the typescript of Murder by Twelve (1935), an unpublished detective story by twelve Wellington literary men.

I've made borrowings from *My Scrip of Joy*, by Lawrence Inch, *Starry Skies*, by A. C. Gifford, *Journalese*, by Robin Hyde, *The Sugarbag Years*, by Tony Simpson, *Art in New Zealand 1928–1934*, several of Pat Lawlor's books and a number of newspaper reports and articles. I'm happy to acknowledge these although I can no longer identify them all.

Several small changes in historical fact have been made to help the story along.

YMARIU (TRUG) ADIFFIA